A ROGUE'S CHRISTMAS

ELIZABETH ESSEX

OLIVER-HEBER BOOKS

A rogue's Christmas Copyright 2024 © Elizabeth Essex

Cover art by Dar Alber at Wicked Smart Designs

Published by Oliver-Heber Books

0 9 8 7 6 5 4 3 2 1

For Judy Cleaver Catanese, to whom my first romance was dedicated fourteen years ago.
For the friendship that has seen us through forty-six years and sustained me through twenty-two books. Every time we have the good fortune to be together,
you fill the room with laughter and my heart with joy.
I wish everyone might have such a friend.

PROLOGUE

*H*e was mad.

He had to be. Because he couldn't seem to stop himself.

Which made him madder, still. He was mad, because at precisely nine o'clock on the evening of December 6th, Miss Flora Conway stepped into the drawing room of Lady Augusta Ivers's Christmastide soirée and everything else—every other sound and person—seemed to fade away, leaving only her.

He knew the exact time, because he consulted his pocket watch, both to mark the moment and to force himself to look away from her. While he imagined a beautiful girl like Miss Conway might be used to the weight of people's wonder, he didn't imagine it was an altogether comfortable burden. Either way, he was determined not to burden her with *his* heavy gaze. He accounted himself too self-disciplined to become some infernal ogler. Even now.

Especially now.

So, he turned away to contemplate a painting, or a sconce, or a bloody crack in the wall. Anything. Anything but her.

But it was impossible.

At nine-sixteen, she undertook a slow, but solitary perambulation of the room—everything graceful and elegant, an aloof swan gliding along a snowy shore. At nine twenty-two, she refused a glass of champagne and sat by herself on a chair along the far wall, having quietly rebuffed any number of people who sought to speak with her. She all but radiated uncharacteristic solitude.

She was, to his acute eye, engaged in the contemplation of some deep thought or problem—a small pleat had formed between the otherwise flawless arch of her golden brows.

Not that he cared exclusively for physical beauty—he had learned the hard way that it was character that counted. But Miss Flora Conway's character had been set for quite some time as being as exemplary as her beauty. She was thoughtful, kind and generous. Everyone said so. Quick to smile and a pleasure to be around. Transparently open and inviting.

Everything he was not. Especially now.

At ten-o-six, she sighed and rearranged her silken skirts, but otherwise did not move. She did not stand. She did not smile. She stared at the floor of Lady Augusta Ivers's drawing room until he could no longer stand it.

And so, at ten twenty-two, after consulting his pocket watch one last time, he cursed his demons, accepted his fate and stepped away from the wall, resolved at last to do something about the fact that he was hopelessly, stupidly and inconveniently in love with Miss Flora Conway— before it was too late to do anything at all.

CHAPTER 1

EDINBURGH, SCOTLAND

SAINT NICHOLAS DAY, DECEMBER, 1802

lora Conway adjusted her posture so as not to crease the lovely silk taffeta of her high-waisted gown—her maid, Raines, had been at some pains to steam the fabric into cascading perfection, and Flora admired and respected the woman's professionalism too much to be careless with her clothes.

But the sad truth was, not even the lovely, glistening, white silk—for there was no other fashionable color at present for young ladies, even in hidebound Scotland, but especially at Christmastide—could lighten her mood. While the whole rest of society was doing its best to be festive and bright despite the ancient ban against celebrations, she was feeling decidedly unsatisfied with the season.

No, not unsatisfied, but restless. Wondering what was next for her. If she had some purpose in this life other than animating other people's salons and ballrooms now that she could not hold any salons of her own.

Her maid, Raines, had, in her inimitable Scots way, called her *peely-wally*, and Flora could only agree. She *felt* peely-wally, off-color and off-center.

Unhappy.

There—she had named it.

"Why, my dear Miss Conway!" The hostess of the soirée, Lady Augusta Ivers, imposed herself upon Flora's field of vision, a tall advent candle of a woman, with her purple satin gown and flaming red hair. "Flora, darling." Lady Ivers clasped her hand and kissed her cheek. "Tell me at once—whatever can be wrong? What on earth are you doing alone?"

"Lady Ivers." Flora rose and pasted on her polite social smile. "You are too kind. What a lovely party." And it was a lovely celebration of the Feast of Saint Nicholas. While from the street, Lady Ivers's townhouse was all restrained elegance, inside, the buffet tables in the dining room practically groaned with platters of food, all manner of meat and fruits and cakes spread from one end of the table to the other.

Which Flora privately thought was a strange way to celebrate a saint who had dedicated his life to serving the sick and suffering and was known for giving his money to the poor—she doubted any poor people were on Lady Ivers's very exclusive guest list.

"A party which you are not enjoying," her hostess insisted. "Come, walk with me and tell me what's wrong."

"Nothing, my lady, I assure you—"

"None of that." Lady Ivers cut her off with a quick tap of her fan. "I know an unhappy girl when I see one. Now tell me, immediately, who has been so careless as to break your heart?"

Flora could only smile at such a suggestion. "I sure you, my lady, not a soul has broken my heart." In her current state of lassitude, she was entertaining no callers and accepting very few invitations. And, upon reflection, she should probably not have accepted this one.

Lady Ivers raised a skeptical eyebrow. "Are you quite sure? For my own part, I would put your father or your sister's name down at the top of the list."

"My sister?" Flora's easy, amused smile faded into careful astonishment. "My sister is my dearest friend and confidante and—"

"And lately married and very happy, judging by the

smiles that wreath her and her new husband's faces! Their delight in each other is nearly indecent." Lady Ivers's own warm smile told Flora that she did not truly believe what she said and was only teasing. "But she no longer has as much time for confidences to share with her sweet sister. You would have every right to perhaps feel alone. Especially with your father gone as well."

Flora opened her mouth to rebut the lady's words but drew in a deep breath instead. Until her sister Maisie's marriage, the avowed purpose of Flora's life had been to see Maisie made happy—a task everyone else had thought impossible. And yet Flora had done it. She had pushed and prodded and plotted and encouraged until nature had finally been allowed to take its inevitable course—Maisie and Archie had fallen madly in love.

But Flora had somehow never thought beyond that. Never planned for what she might want to come after. And although she had tried to act as if Papa's disgrace and resignation from his position as Lord Advocate had not been a grievous shock, her own accompanying loss of stature within society had been, if not exactly distressing, then certainly revealing.

Society, even in thorny, contrary Scotland, had two different sets of rules for women, depending upon their age and beauty. Though Flora might be accounted beautiful, and was certainly young, with her father now gone, she was judged by a witheringly strict code of conduct. She was looked at askance and treated as an unfortunate, despite having done nothing untoward herself.

Yet, she had steadfastly resisted all suggestions to shore up her position within society by hiding herself away in remorse—*she* had done nothing wrong! And she refused to bolster her respectability by taking on a companion. She was too independent for genteel companionship. Too used to being in charge to let anyone else take over.

It was a damnably quelling thing to have charge of oneself but be censored for it.

So, Lady Ivers was, she supposed, right. "Am I so transparent?"

"Only to me," Lady Ives assured her quietly. "Only to the people who care about you."

The hidden heaviness in Flora's heart rose to become a lump in her throat. "You are very kind."

"I am not," the lady rejoined with mock disdain. "And you are expressly forbidden from saying so. I am not kind—I am Machiavellian and I can't have one of the most beautiful, most sought-after young ladies in all of Edinburgh making a wallflower of herself in my drawing room. It won't do."

"I don't suppose it will," Flora agreed on a sigh. But she certainly didn't feel sought-after. She felt…different. Removed from all the festive gaiety. Too disappointed to enjoy herself. Too independent to join into the spirit of the holidays.

She felt…impossible.

She should have stayed home. St. Nicholas's Day ought to be a time for families leaving gifts for each other in shoes or stockings and exchanging other small tokens of affection and warmth, such as knitted mittens, embroidered handkerchiefs or ginger sweets the way she and Maisie, used to. But Maisie had a new home of her own now, with her new husband, Archie, and Flora imagined the two of them were following St. Nicholas's example more closely, by feeding hundreds of poor souls who lived—if it could be called living—in the closes that ran beneath the old city like ribs from a spine.

"Forgive me, my lady, but—"

"I will forgive you if you come with me now and let me introduce you to several young men—and a few slightly older ones," the lady added meaningfully. "For you know how profitable such an alliance can be."

Lady Ivers herself was the independent relic of a much older naval man to whom she was said to have been devoted, going to sea with him for years at a time. When Admiral Ivers died, he left his lady a stylishly rich young widow—although she never remarried, wearing lavender as a sign of her continued grief and devotion to her beloved late husband.

Her example was almost enough to make Flora believe in true love. Almost.

But true love seemed to be rarer than Scots Dumpy hen's teeth. To Lady Ivers's wealthy, influential, titled guests, love was a mere afterthought to marriage—fine if it happened, but equally fine if it did not. To them, marriage was all about advantage, not affection.

It was a dull, stupid life that left young women like her with so few chances that weren't *being judged* for advantages and *being chosen* as a wife.

And which was worse, Flora had only recently come to understand that she had been bred—brought up and educated by her father—for the sole purpose of just such a trade. She wasn't like Maisie—so full of passion and conviction and talent that she could make a life outside the dictates of society. Flora felt she had no profession but charm, no accomplishments but her given beauty.

"So." Augusta Ivers tapped her fan against her palm, eying her drawing room as if she were a general surveying the field of battle. "What do I have of handsome young men?"

Flora followed her gaze but there was nothing new to see—no one she hadn't seen before. No one who might be interested in her as a person, not just as a candidate for the position of wife.

It was all too dull. All too predictable. All too disappointing.

"No, thank you, my lady." Flora firmed her voice. And her resolve. "I find I'm beginning to enjoy my independence." As limited as that independence might be. But there was one thing she could still choose for herself. "I've come to the conclusion that marriage just isn't for me."

CHAPTER 2

"*F*lora, darling." Lady Ivers laughed even as she chided. "That's fine, but let us speak plainly—have you enough money to remain unmarried? It is an expensive thing, an independent spinsterhood."

"Money?" This Flora had not contemplated. Until this moment, she had never questioned Papa's wealth. Or imagined that wealth might not continue to provide for her. "I don't know."

"Well, you need to know," Lady Ivers counseled. "I know it is crass to speak of money, but it would behoove you to get an accurate accounting of how things lay."

Flora had been instructed by her father to visit his bankers on the Mound on a monthly basis for her household expenses while he was away. But she had never questioned the white-haired clerk as to the solvency of said account, nor asked if there were any other accounts her father might have left behind while he went off plant-hunting to India—or wherever it was he was traveling.

How foolish.

Flora was disappointed anew—in herself. "I will do so immediately, my lady. Thank you."

"We ladies need to look after one another," was Lady Ivers's opinion. "The world is not made for us, so we must remake it as and where we can. But as to independence..." She spoke quietly. "Have you considered someone older? Not to put too fine a point upon it, but someone more likely to pass on long before you?" She favored Flora with an ironic smile. "Widowhood has a great deal to recommend it."

"Independence and the lack of a husband being the chief amongst the recommendations?"

Lady Ivers patted Flora's hand. "This is why I like you—you're smart as a whip and have no pretenses about it." She narrowed her gaze at the assembly. "Now let us see if we can find someone who is well past the spring season of his life. What about the Marques de San Adrian?" Lady Ivers indicated a tall, dark, impeccably dressed gentleman with white hair and black glossy boots, across the room. "He is handsome enough for you, I'll judge. But do you speak any Spanish?"

Flora tried for a brief moment to picture herself in

an aristocratic *cigarral* in the foothills of sunny Spain. "No."

"Then perhaps not." Lady Ivers moved swiftly on. "Ah, the Earl of Knole is newly widowed. But there are the children—four, I believe. And grown."

"I have no objection to children—in principle." Flora tried to be polite. "But I do have grave reservations about a man who would make me stepmother to a woman older than myself." She cast her glance meaningfully at the earl's eldest daughter.

"Quite right," Lady Ivers agreed. "One's own children are one thing, but other people's children are another matter entirely and ought to be approached with caution."

"Or not at all," Flora rejoined honestly before recalling herself to politeness. "I beg your pardon, my lady."

Lady Ivers took no offense. "You'll note I have no children—aside from my most beloved niece. By choice, not circumstance, I might add. We never wanted babies, the Admiral and I. I never wanted to share him with anyone besides his first love, the Royal Navy!" Her smile was perhaps a bit misty even as she teased. "But that reminiscence prompts me to think I might tempt you with a career military man. There's a sort of widowhood that comes from having a husband away on active duty —an admirable situation for an independent spirit."

"I hadn't thought of that," Flora admitted. "I do find I rather like being on my own." Mostly. She liked the independence of running her own house and catering to her own needs and tastes, instead of Papa's. But running the house wasn't enough. It wasn't a true *purpose.*

"Excellent" Lady Ivers encouraged. "Perhaps Colonel Crathie, there? Commands a regiment of horse. Has most of his hair and all of his teeth. Not a bad prospect," she judged. "He's perhaps not a great intellect, but he's likable enough. The right woman will make a better man of him."

"Lady Ivers, I beg you would not abuse your company this way," a deep Scots voice from behind them interrupted. "That man is nothing but a bag of pants."

Flora was astonished—and vastly amused—to find the speaker was a tall, handsome, deeply tanned man with burnished hair. At the sight of him, something within her chest kicked over, like a horse trying to free itself from its harness traces.

But what a strange feeling—and what a strange way to describe it. Flora had never kicked over anything in her life. Avoided, perhaps, tiptoed around, certainly, or even edged by carefully. But never, ever kicked—it was too self-indulgent.

"Hah! Jack, darling," Lady Ivers enthused, turning her cheek to accept the fellow's kiss. "Speak of the devil and up he pops, right on cue. Lovely to see you, as always." Lady Ivers waved her fan in the fellow's direction before she said to Flora, "You know Jack Balfour, I'm sure. Everyone knows Jack."

"We are acquainted," the man acknowledged with a civil bow.

Flora belatedly realized that she had indeed been introduced to the man—at her father's very first 'salon' for the great and good of Edinburgh, last winter. The night she had discovered Maisie in Archie Carrington's arms. The night everything that had eventually culminated in Papa losing favor as the Lord Advocate had been set in motion.

Flora had clearly forgotten this remarkably attractive fellow in the whirlwind of events that followed. He was Jonathan Balfour, her exacting memory recalled, a captain of the Royal Navy, looking everything cynical but somehow urbane out of his naval uniform.

Yet, despite the cynical smile, there was...something about him. Something sad in the set of his mouth. Something weary in the cast of his gray eyes that drew her attention and gave her pause, all at the same time.

He crossed his arms over his chest, and she found herself staring at his brown hands, for no reason that she could fathom. Perhaps it was the way he held himself—a little stiffly, with a wary sort of attentiveness, as if he had gotten too used to the feel of his ship rising and falling underfoot and now found the solid oak of Lady Ivers's parquet unsettling.

Not for the first time that evening, Flora wished her sister were there. Maisie would no doubt find Captain Balfour an interesting subject for a portrait—he was fairly bristling with character. And only a portraitist of Maisie's talent could capture the banked fire of the captain's steely gaze.

Which he turned on her now. "Miss Conway." The captain's look seemed to skate over her in only brief acknowledgment before he turned away. "What are you up to, Augusta?"

"Introducing my dear Miss Conway to some of my other gentlemen guests—"

"Crathie? Bag. Of. Pants," he repeated.

Augusta Ivers laughed and shook her head as she turned back to Flora. "Jack is full of these marvelous witticisms. He's quite the rogue. I don't know if you've heard that our captain is now the Earl of Kinloch, for his sins and for all the good it's done him. But, I will warn you—as I will also warn him—that you're not for him. Despite the title—or perhaps because of it. He's poor."

Well. Flora was astonished to find she had been wrong—there was at least one poor person at the party, after all.

And she, who had not known about Captain Balfour's elevation to the peerage—and who could now see that what she thought had been cynicism in the man's face, was in fact, a combustible combination of rage and grief—was so very much surprised that she spoke, for the first time in the whole of her adult life, without thinking.

"How…regrettable."

CHAPTER 3

*J*ack felt he could have choked on the pity in her voice. But rather than voice his own damnable regrets at inheriting a bankrupt earldom, he adopted the careless mask that kept the world at large at bay. "Nothing to be done about it, I'm afraid," he quipped.

"Nothing but go back to sea," Lady Ivers averred.

The Divine Miss Conway, she of the piercing blue eyes and golden, angelic hair, sent him a frowning gaze from under her feathery lashes. "Go back to the Navy? But why? Will the peace with France not hold?"

Miss Conway would be as astute as she was beautiful. "The Treaty of Amiens has held—thus far," Jack explained with a world-weary sort of shrug. "But peace is a fragile thing that must be waged as aggressively as war. Perhaps more so. But, yes, if the Navy will have me back, now that I'm a useless nob, I will certainly go." He dismissed the whole of the aristocracy, as well as the entirety of the Royal Navy—including his long and storied career as a successful frigate captain—with a wave. "I'll have to go hat in hand to the Admiralty in London a-begging."

Miss Conway nodded and tipped her head aside with a solemn sort of smile. "Ah. I understand. You'll have to be *chosen*."

Well, damn her sparkling eyes. She would be as thoughtful as she was astute. Not that he minded being chosen—it would prove a relief to be judged for his merit rather than selected by his bloodline. But there was something about the way she said it—something too like pity to leave him any less uncomfortable.

"Nonsense," Augusta Ivers conveniently disagreed. "The Admiralty know a useful man when they see him—and count their share of his prize monies. But I do hate to think you'll be a tottering old man by the time you win another fortune like the last—if you're not put to bed with a cannonball first." She sighed. "And even if you do, the estate will probably gobble that fortune up for debts, same as the first."

He barely felt the pang of regret for the years of dangerous toil it had taken to earn himself his own independent fortune through prize monies—and at the speed with which the money had been summarily consumed by the earldom's outstanding financial obligations—so familiar was the feeling now.

But Miss Conway's lofted brows told him she had not been apprised of his sad tale. Then again, perhaps the story of how Jack had come to inherit nothing but a moldering pile of bricks and debts was old news by now.

Or perhaps she had been too consumed with her own sad tale—her father's recent fall from favor as the Lord Advocate had been as sudden as his ascent to the plummy post had been in the first place. And rumor had it that her own sister, Maisie Conway, the storied portraitist who was now Lady Carrington, had been a party to that downfall—Lord Carrington certainly had been in his role as the editor of the political quarterly, The Edinburgh Review.

Perhaps that was empathy he saw behind Flora Conway's sparkling blue eyes.

No. He could not allow it to be. Augusta had already warned him off once. He should not require another telling.

Flora Conway was not for him.

He might not have any money, but he still had his pride. "I'm not so old as to be approaching tottering, Augusta."

The lady smiled her disagreement and moved on to other concerns. "But surely, you'll not attempt the journey to London before the end of the festive season? Nothing will be decided during Christmastide—even the almighty Admiralty turns soft and soporific for the season. There's no sense in your going before Epiphany at the earliest."

Jack knew she was right. But if there was one thing he could not abide, it was inaction. Or pity. "I needs must attend to Kinloch as well. I cannot always be propping up your walls for you, my dear Lady Ivers."

"No, I must have you more useful than that," Lady Ivers agreed on a narrow laugh. "And to that point—I cannot have our dear, sweet Flora sitting alone with no one to entertain her. But while you are arguably one of the most entertaining men in Scotland, Jack dear, you know you simply won't do. You're far too much the rogue."

Jack didn't mind being damned by such offhand praise—what was one more damnation in the face of so many? "Be that as it may, why do you persist in this ludicrous parade of ne'er do wells?" He gestured economically but dismissively to Colonel Crathie as a stand-in for the collective bags of pants on display.

"What are you talking about—ne'er-do-wells?" Augusta Ivers blustered, playfully rapping her fan against his chest. "I'll have you know there's not a single ne'er-do-well amongst my invitation lists," she insisted. "Solvent to a man—with the exception of you. You can count upon me to be attentive to such important things, my dear Flora. I should never be so negligent as to offer you an acquaintance who was not everything aboveboard."

Jack made an inelegant sound of derision.

"Well," Augusta began to admit, "you may be right, Jack—everyone is aboveboard but *you*."

He could only smile, even as he offered his riposte. "Pray offer the poor lass something more than a head of hair and a mouth of teeth. A man for her will need to be a great deal more than an old windbag like Crathie. I wouldn't trust his arse with a fart much less a woman of Miss Conway's caliber."

Something in the divine Miss Conway's expression —the slight pleating at the corners of her mouth, along with a sunrise sort of warmth that rose across her cheeks before she smoothed her face into blander politeness—showed that he had done his part to amuse her whilst he had rather crudely warned her off.

And yet, she surprised him with a little sidelong glance. "I thank you for the compliment, but for myself, I should think that neither a windbag nor a bag of pants is as good as a bag of money. One can certainly be too poor, but one can never be too rich."

Jack wanted to laugh out loud—he hadn't expected such wit. "You could have any rich man you wanted." He gestured to the room. "All you have to is aim your swivel gun of a smile at them to make it so."

"A swivel gun, is it? Such favor," she teased with a smile. "You think it really is that easy?"

He knew it was—he had been slain by her smile at a cable's length, without ever having spoken to her before. "Aye. It is so."

The damned clever lass aimed that dangerously sublime smile at him. "Any man, you say? Any man but *you*, Lord Kinloch?"

"Captain," he injected stupidly in some desperate effort to mitigate the sting of his desperate—and desperately vain—attraction. "I prefer Captain Balfour, Miss Conway," he said in a lower, calmer tone. "For that title, I earned for myself on my own merit. As did the first Balfours, who were nothing more than pirates and rogues, though successful ones."

Her solemn smile returned in all its bittersweet glory. "It must be a very satisfying thing to be accomplished."

It was. Next to making her smile, it was the only satisfaction left to him. But saying so would never do. "I should be better satisfied by being rich rather than accomplished."

"Would you really?" She looked openly skeptical—he was surprised to find it suited her, this keenness. "For my own part, if I could only have one without the other,

I should infinitely prefer the accomplishment. And your accomplishments in your profession led to your money, did they not?"

The look she gave him—a look that somehow saw straight through the cynical, uncaring veneer he had donned like armor—warned him not to lie. God help him, it was impossible. He could feel himself starting to actually *like* her—her, Flora Conway, the young woman speaking to him, rather that the idealized paragon he had imagined from across the room.

It would never do. "For *my* own part, the accomplishments were all for the sake of getting rich," he said. The money he had earned in hard-fought naval prizes should have freed him to have an independent life, free of the constraints of both his family and his profession. It wasn't that he didn't like being a navy man, it was just that after eighteen years of service, he was bloody tired of putting himself in harm's way for a country that seemed indifferent to the sacrifice.

Despite his cynical tone, she seemed to have heard something of what he was so off-handedly trying to conceal. "The earldom has taken *all* the prize money you earned in the Navy?"

The depth of his regret was so deep he could drown in it. "Every last farthing, Miss Conway. Gone for debts I didn't even have the pleasure of accruing myself. But enough tragedy. All work and no play has made Jack a dull boy, so let us end this unsupportable segue into the sins of the past."

"Certainly," she agreed with the same solemn thoughtfulness before she turned and met his eyes. "For my own part, I had so much rather think of the sins of the future."

CHAPTER 4

*B*eside her, Captain Jack Balfour nearly choked upon his drink. "Miss Conway," he finally said when he recovered himself. "You astonish me."

No more than she had astonished herself. She wasn't quite sure what had come over her, other than this surprising feeling of wanting to amuse and engage him —this cynical, handsome, interesting man who had been declared *not for* her.

Yet as much as she admired Lady Ivers, who was *she* to choose for Flora? Who was anyone to say who she might, or might not, choose for herself? And what she chose, was enter into the slightly sardonic style of the conversation—to amuse herself by flirting. "I like to keep the score even if I can."

He took another sidelong glance at her. "I didn't know we were playing."

Flora gave Jack Balfour what she hoped was a leveling look. "Did you not? A man of your wit and experience? Come now, Captain."

"However much I should like"—Jack Balfour lowered his voice so no one but she might hear him mutter—"to *come* right now—" He was stopped by a sharp rap from Lady Ivers's attentive fan, before he corrected himself. "I fear I must decline. Lady Ivers has fired her warning shot across my bow, and her next will likely put a hole in my hull. So, I beg you will leave me what little pride I have left to my name, and let me withdraw from the line of battle—or rather, return to it, where, with what little luck I have left to my name, I will go aboard some frigate or another to make another fortune that the earldom will swallow whole and still be left hungry."

"Indeed, you will." Lady Ivers squeezed his hand in assurance and affection, clearly glad of the chance to steer the conversation into calmer waters. "You shall earn yourself another fortune to rival the first. That's why I like you."

"You like me because Admiral Ivers found me useful," he countered. "God rest his soul."

"God rest him," the lady echoed with feeling. "I miss him every day. He loved you, Jack. He found you useful because you *were* useful—dutiful, determined, insightful and courageous. I find you useful because you are also wonderfully decorative. Even without any money, you do fill out drawing room quite nicely."

Balfour smiled despite himself. "I live to serve, my lady."

"And so do I. I will write what letters I can to the Admiralty in support of your cause. But until such time as you have a ship to go off to—" She glanced speculatively from the captain to Flora. "Don't let me catch you drawing any more of my ire by flirting so outrageously that you make my darling Miss Conway fall madly in love with you."

Flora was not sure which of them was more shocked —she just stared at Lady Ivers, but Balfour actually guffawed. Which piqued her pride in a way his previous banter had not. "I am perfectly able to defend myself from the captain's wit, my lady."

"My darling Flora." Lady Ivers clasped her hand solicitously. "I know you cut your teeth on London's bachelors, but I beg you will proceed with caution where a rogue like Jack is concerned. Handsome and witty is a powerful combination and when you add in the rest…" She gestured to his admittedly fine person, from his burnished head, down past his handsome face to his large but well-polished boots, before she threw her hands up in animated despair. "All that damnable charm!"

He did indeed possess a damnable amount of charm —to which Flora knew she was not impervious. She had liked her charming brother-in-law, Archie Carrington, almost instantly—far earlier than Maisie, who was much less susceptible to Archie's particular brand of cheek, though she had eventually succumbed.

But Flora had her own charms to wield as her weapons.

And Lady Ivers clearly had eyes in her head. "Well, you can't say I haven't warned you." The lady wagged her fan at the two of them. "Be good! And for God's sake, be smarter than you are good." And with that, the good lady fixed them each with her sternest glare and left them standing alone together.

"Well." Flora was chagrinned to feel her face flame. "I haven't been told off like that since—" She plied her fan to cool her cheeks. "Well, since forever." Her father had rarely corrected Flora, preferring to save his instruction for her sister, Maisie. A glance told her Captain Balfour had weathered the storm of embarrassment more easily than she. "You?"

"Typically, I'm the one delivering the dressing downs, not receiving them," he admitted with a rueful smile that hitched up one corner of his otherwise stern mouth. "But I'll admit I've never had the dubious pleasure of watching a young lady be warned off me before. Quite a novel experience, this."

It was the irreverent pleasure in his smile that encouraged her. "You're enjoying yourself."

"I admit, I am. Far more than I imagined."

"And what had you imagined?"

He hesitated, and then turned himself toward her, so they were shoulder to shoulder as well as eye to eye. "That I would not like you this much."

It was as if everything within her—her heart, lungs, the very blood in her veins—stopped and started and fell apart and came crashing together in one silent instant.

Flora found her mouth open and closed it. And instructed herself to breathe. And then ventured, "You *like* me?"

"Aye," he answered quite simply, as if it weren't the most astonishing thing in the world. "Another novel experience."

"Is it?" She could barely put two words together— she, who had never in her life before this evening, been at a loss for words.

"Damn my eyes, yes," he admitted. But then, as if he thought he had said too much, he donned his cynicism as if it were a comfortable old sea cloak. "When you're older and more experienced, you'll know that. Truly likable people are few and far between in this world."

"Are they?" she asked, feeling instinctively that such a thing could not be true—she had met wonderful, likable people everywhere she had turned in their adopted city.

She felt compelled to combat his cynicism. "And are you so very old and experienced? Despite your appearance —" His face was certainly weathered, and his clothing was worn—shiny at the collar and cuffs—though his bottle green coat was immaculately tailored. "—I gather you cannot be more than thirty or five and thirty."

"I am indeed thirty," he confirmed quietly, "while you cannot be more than one and twenty."

Flora could do nothing but own her years. "Nearly twenty-two. Though I am not so naive or unworldly as such an age might imply." She had come into something approaching adulthood at the tender, but bristlingly aware age of fourteen, when she had first understood the injustices foisted upon her sister as a result of her physical limitations. And then, as Lady Ivers had affirmed, she had cut her teeth on London's bachelors— though she had never been tempted or troubled or amused—or so thoroughly engaged—by one of them the way she was now.

"Indeed?" Balfour agreed in the same evenhanded, but subtly cynical tone. "Most young women are married at your *advanced* age. I admit to some curiosity as to why you are not?"

"Yes, I'm absolutely ancient." She entered into the spirit of his tease. "Best fetch me a Bath chair to roll me about. That will surely catch me a husband." She found she liked matching wits with him. And making him smile. But she liked astonishing him more. "For my own part, I want purpose far more than I want a husband."

Balfour's brow lofted in a perfect arch. "I'm sure it ought to be easy enough to devote yourself to some worthy cause." His eyes skated away, though, as if he was regretting speaking so openly. Or, worse, was growing bored.

And so, Flora took her courage in hand, and said exactly what she wanted to say. "But it is not easy at all. At the moment, I'm trying to decide if *you're* a worthy cause, Captain."

She had his attention now—his frown grew slowly fierce, creasing his brow as he tried to divine her meaning. She decided to help him along. "I've decided to follow your example and choose my own fate."

"My dear Miss Conway," he answered with a wry shake of his head. "In my experience, it is fate who has done all the choosing."

"Oh, no," she disagreed. "I dislike this idea of an unseen hand as the force that is moving us through this world. It is nothing more than fate that you excelled at your career?"

He pulled a thoughtful face, his mouth turning down at the corners. "I suppose I chose to apply myself and excel, but as I was twelve at the time my career was chosen for me, I cannot claim any agency in the act. My miserly Scots father chose for us all, my brothers and I—

put us into His Majesty's service when we were but lads, probably so he wouldn't have to spend any money to feed us himself. He chose the Royal Navy for me, the Royal Marines for my younger brother, and His Majesty's Army for the eldest, the best of us, who ought to have been spared from service, but was not. Duncan had the great misfortune to fall at Castlebar, thus making me the heir. If that isn't fate, I don't know what is."

Was this the source of his cynicism, this anger at the choices that had been thrust upon him? How sad. "I am very sorry for your loss."

"As am I. But as my family's parting gift to me was a bankrupt earldom, I hope you will forgive me my lack of enthusiasm for the title."

"I do," she said simply. "And even if you needs must return to the navy, I hope it gives you a great deal of satisfaction to know your own merit the way you do."

He was still for a long moment before his discomfort reasserted itself. "Forgive me. I did not mean to boast."

"You did not," she answered truthfully. "Your merit is a matter of common knowledge, known to anyone who reads the naval dispatches in the newspapers."

"You read the newspapers, do you?" His tone returned to teasing. "I would never have guessed Miss Conway was a secret Bluestocking."

She was no intellect, but she found she liked his

image of her. "I like to be well-informed about the events of the day." Such knowledge had mattered a great deal more when her father had been Lord Advocate. Now she simply read to please herself. "And I am in the fortunate position of having no one to forbid me."

"Were you once forbidden?" He looked at her rather more intently than he had before.

Flora wasn't sure of his purpose. "Not exactly. But censured, certainly."

"And you read anyway," he answered for himself, as a smile spread slowly across his lips like warm marmalade across a buttered bun. "What else do you do that's forbidden, Miss Conway?"

Something within—her restlessness and dissatisfaction at the choices that were available to her, combined with the curious effect of that improbably mischievous smile—set the skin of her palms to tingling.

"I talk to impecunious men," she answered with an arch smile. "For no other purpose than to enjoy myself immensely."

"Is this your sin of the future, Miss Conway? Amusing yourself with me because you've been forbidden to?"

She had never thought of herself as a defiant type, but perhaps she had been too compliant in her efforts to mitigate her sister's very reasonable defiance. "I am trying to amuse you, Captain," she answered honestly.

"Because of all the things I cannot choose, I *can* choose this."

Balfour stood very still, looking out at the assembly with that cynical detachment. As if he were thinking of anything other than her.

But she was wrong.

Because he finally turned to her and said, "Then, my dear Miss Conway, I feel compelled to say, that if *I* were able to choose, I should only ever choose you."

CHAPTER 5

*J*ack disciplined himself to breathe. Evenly. In and out. Not to let his face heat like a slow match. Or worse, go ashen and sea grey from the absolute stupidity of expressing his most private thoughts in this utterly exposing way.

Beside him, Miss Conway was just as still and watchful, barely breathing herself. But she finally took in a long breath and focused her attention solely on him. And then she smiled—a smile of such revelatory wonder that Jack felt the fullness of her charm settle upon him like a sunbeam. And he knew he was lost. That he would do anything to feel the warmth of her regard. Anything. Everything.

"Then pray tell me, my dear Captain," she spoke so quietly he found himself bending toward her to hear. "How might we go about making that happen?"

Jack heard the words, but feared they could not be true. His sense of responsibility, his honor demanded that he had misheard her. She could not mean what he wanted her to mean. "Pray don't toy with me, Miss Conway." His voice was as low as his hopes. "Poor and unimportant as I am, I am not a plaything."

"Do I appear to be the type of person who would toy with another's attention or affections?" she asked with that solemn honestly of hers. "Because I assure you, I am not."

She did not, in fact, look like the type of person who might toy with anyone, at all, for any reason. It was one of the reasons he *liked* her.

"No," he finally said. "And neither am I, so I will say again what needs to be said—and understood. I am poor. I am leaving."

"I understand, Captain." She nodded, her eyes never leaving his face. "And what I would like to know in return, is, if you are the sort of person who is careless with your words or admiration?"

He was, despite his cynical protestations to indifference, both a sworn officer and a gentleman who knew both his duty and what was right. "I assure you I am not."

"Then," she said simply as if she had made up her mind. "What comes next? Right now. This evening. Before you must go away."

It was as if the floor beneath his feet had shifted—he was immediately at sea and unprepared for the feeling of being so summarily tossed to and fro.

Privacy comes next, was his only thought, though there was little privacy to be found at such a public event in such a private home—he could hardly avail himself of Lady Ivers's bed chamber.

And she could not mean what he wanted her to mean. She could not.

Jack took a moment to straighten his coat and cuffs to allow himself to regain his metaphorical balance. To make sure he had not imagined the entirety of the conversion from out of the depth of his wildest longings. "A walk," he offered more reasonably. "A slow promenade so we might..." Might not immediately proceed to some conveniently darkened corner of the library where he might taste the sweet tartness of her wit from her lips. "...further our discussion."

"Perhaps a dance might be easier?" she suggested with a glance at some of the younger guests who were forming into the lines of a country dance.

Nothing could be less to his advantage. "I beg you will not put me through the torture, Miss Conway. I am a naval man, not a dandy."

She gave him one of her sweetly solemn smiles. "If you could learn the particulars of every sail and spar for the furtherance of your career, sir, I feel certain you could overcome the far more mundane complexities of a country dance."

In Jack's mind, dancing was but a poor substitution for another activity wherein a man and a woman exercised face to face. But he was determined to keep his less than gentlemanly demons battened down and weather reefed. "One might think," he allowed, "though I have never had the time or tuition. I was sent into the Navy before my father could be taxed with finding a dancing instructor."

Flora Conway let out a low little hum of laughter, that made him think of honeybees and flowers and other idiocies in the middle of winter, before she began to walk with him—although he made sure to measure his steps to match hers—and asked, "May I propose a more interesting alternative?"

Whatever it was, it could not be merely interesting. It would be maddening. And damned inconvenient. Because no matter what she suggested, he knew he would do it, as sure as the tide. "Aye."

"There!" Her smile was full of satisfaction. "Now you sound like both a proper Scot and a sea captain. And not that you don't look entirely distinguished, but may I ask, why are we not treated to the sight of you in your rather dashing uniform?"

It was another boon to his damnable pride that she remembered their first meeting—which was precisely the last time he had had the comfort of wearing his post captain's uniform. "Custom forbids the wearing of His Majesty's uniform while being off post. Simply put—no ship, no uniform. And I have no ship at present, courtesy of my being forced to tend to the exigencies of the earldom."

"This I did not know," she acknowledged. "So many interesting things to learn."

So many more interesting things he might teach her. If she were truly willing.

God knew she looked able.

No, he must not think like that. He must remember he was at a private, Christmastide soirée with a young lady of good family who was *not for him*.

So, he and the lass who was not for him took a few more silent turns of the room before Flora Conway very gently laid her hand against his forearm—which obligingly raised itself up to take the subtle weight of her elegantly gloved arm—and just as subtly, steered them through the nearest door, then down the staircase beyond.

Jack allowed himself to be led. She set a course for the back of the house where a small glass conservatory housed an abundance of tender, exotic plants from Lady Ivers's travels about the world with her naval husband. Greenery, such as potted palms, abounded despite the season, while a very old grape vine reached its bare, arthritic fingers in a lattice up the slanted glass roof.

"I've always liked this room," he said to allay his inexplicable rush of nerves. He had faced down the enemy French and Spanish, for God's sake—surely, he could converse with an attractive, witty, insightful young woman without acting like the greenest landsman. "The Admiral liked to sit and take his coffee here when he was home." He gestured to a comfortable divan and armchair at the near end of the room where a single glass lamp stood ready to illuminate the dark, but Jack left it unlit, exorcising his demons by moving away from her down the length of the room. He moored up against the glass, where a large fern pressed its tender fronds against the icy pane. "He used to say he liked being able to see the stars the way he was used to at sea."

"What a lovely thought." Miss Conway looked up at the dark night sky twinkling through the glass. "For the longest time, I had no idea there was a glasshouse attached to this house. It's a lovely sort of hidden jewel. Reminds me of home."

"The house on Kirk Brae Head?" he asked. The old Jacobean house at the west end of the New Town had been the Widow Fraser's before the Conway family had taken up residence. The Conways had filled the place with the elder daughter's elegant art, but the darker, older, more formal style of the house had never suggested to Jack the sort of airy, but lush, domestic ease the Ivers conservatory offered.

"No," she answered, though she smiled. "I was thinking of our house back in Richmond, along the river in England, before we came here. It felt warm and green and easy, much like this room. Not this perpetual grey winter we seem to have here in Scotland."

He had not thought her so particularly English, so seamlessly had she immersed herself in Edinburgh society—and subsequently sailed straight into his over-active admiration. "I apologize on Scotland's behalf."

"You're very kind." She smiled at him—the glint of her white teeth winking at him in the dim light. "But that will be our secret—that you're secretly kind."

Damn his eyes. How could she be as keen and witty and insightful as she was beautiful? It ought to be impossible. "You've found me out."

"Have I?" She tipped her head to one side. "I can't imagine you're the sort of man one can find out so easily. In fact, I should think you wear this charming cynicism of yours much the way you would your naval uniform—like a well-worn friend."

Impossible. "My dear Miss Conway, you *have* found me out."

"I rather wish I *were* your dear Miss Conway. Dear enough for you to call me Flora. Because I should like to call you Jack. It has a nice ring to it."

Her straightforward compliments came one after another, seemingly innocuous, until they were a billowing weight piled upon him. He had no defense against such soft arts. "Miss Conway, I beg you."

"I was rather hoping I wasn't going to have to beg." She looked only fleetingly chagrinned. She tipped her head to the side in that solemnly sweet way of hers, and he was all but gone. "But if I have to, I will."

CHAPTER 6

*H*it again and again with soft but lethal shots. At this rate it wouldn't take the French to put him to bed with a cannonball—Miss Flora Conway would see him consigned to the deep with her fatally sweet frankness. He would be well advised to find a way back to safe harbor.

Instead, he moved nearer. "What an astonishingly way of flirting, you have, Miss Conway."

"Flora," she repeated with quiet insistence. "And I am very glad to find we *are* flirting."

"I am not flirting with you, Miss Conway," he asserted, using the shelter of the dark foliage to hide his lie. "I am attempting to understand why you are flirting with me." Why a woman of her caliber would have anything to do with him on so slight a temptation as his charm. He had never, in all his months of observing her, seen this sort of singular attention in her. She had always been engaging, but he had never seen her lower her chin and gaze up at someone the way she was doing now. "Why a young woman of your beauty and understanding and solvency would want to have anything to do with a man of my poverty."

She looked up at him, her eyes as luminous as beacons, her smile as soft and dangerous as a shoal. "Because you're *interesting*."

"Miss Conway, I beg you." He tried one last time. "You know nothing of me. I could be a spy for the damn French, for all you know."

That suggestion astonished her—she drew back, frowning, as if she were trying to see him better in the dim light. And then her face cleared. "I think if you were, you would not be so poor."

Impossible. "You really have found me out, Miss Conway. But you must not think—"

"What I think, is that you intrigue me, Captain."

Oh, that was infinitely treacherous. And infinitely promising. "My dear Miss Conway, you must not persist in this determination to see the best in everyone—especially when there is no good to be found. It is a terrible characteristic."

"So noted." She smiled with a sort of impish delight. "And you are a *terrible* cynic—terrible because, deep down, you don't want to be so cynical, do you?"

More treacherous still. Deep down, he wanted impossible things. "My dear Miss Conway—"

"Oh, no." She held up her hand. "Don't attempt that pedantic tone with me, for I have seen behind the veil and there is no unseeing. You, Captain Balfour, penniless Earl of Kinloch, are a secret idealist. And perhaps even—" She paused for effect. "Even a romantic."

"Miss Conway," he protested.

She cut off his lament with a wave. "Flora. And don't bother. I won't believe you. You use cynicism to hide your true self. To arm yourself against the slings and arrows of outrageous fortune—which, I admit in your case, have been extraordinarily outrageous."

There was nothing he could say—no protest that might ring true. Because she was right—he wouldn't be so damned cynical if the world didn't keep letting him down. If it didn't keep forcing mediocrity upon him—and everyone else, too. "Only madmen could live in this world and be their true selves."

She reached out impulsively to touch his hand. "And you are a little mad, I think. Mad enough to care."

Damn his eyes. The slight weight of her hand nearly tipped him over. He felt utterly upended, as if sand was shifting under his feet, even as he tried to shoal himself up.

"I am mad." He proved it by turning so that they faced each other, standing so close that his legs brushed against her skirts, so he could indulge in his latest folly —raising her hand to his lips and bestowing upon her small, gloved knuckles, a kiss. "Mad enough to do as you want and flirt with you. And anything else you might ask of me."

"Go on." Her voice was the barest whisper.

"Shall I?" He lowered his voice to match hers, everything intimate and confidential. "Shall I tell you what I think you really want with me, Miss Conway?"

"I want…" She swallowed and took a shallow breath, but she did not look away. "First—for you to call me Flora."

"Lass," he teased. He let his hand brush against the soft satin of her skirts, barely causing a ripple. And yet he knew she felt it because she sighed and shifted—into the wake of his touch, not away.

"Is it so hard to say a name?"

Damn his eyes, yes. It was too hard. Too intimate. Too soon. Somehow, for all the time he had wasted watching her from afar, he was loath to hurry her along. Even now. Especially now. "Far too difficult. I am a simple sailor, lass, and not a poet to recite sonnets to your name."

"I need no poems, Captain. Nor promises, either."

Deeper waters, still. "You are beautiful enough to inspire them. Surely you know that?"

She shrugged, an elegant little hitch of her satin-clad

shoulder. "Beauty is as beauty does, my sister used to say." She drew back enough to strip off her evening gloves, though she kept hold of them, slowly throttling them to death.

It was good to know she was as at sea as he.

"I cannot take any credit for being beautiful as I had nothing to do with it," she went on. "It is certainly not an accomplishment."

He tried a different, but no less true, compliment. "You are as insightful as you are beautiful."

A hint of a smile warmed her lips. "Then perhaps I may take credit for the insight, although it was my sister who helped me—rather forcefully at times—to form my character and my intellect."

He could not picture Flora Conway being forced to do anything she did not want to do—she seemed too…. Too much herself to be a subject to persuasion. "Time well spent."

"Thank you." She graced him with the sunrise of her smile and the chill in the room seemed to retreat a little. "As I hope this time will be with you."

The tide had already turned within him, the current of attraction was too strong to resist. Jack squared his feet to feel more on solid ground, because despite every gentlemanly instinct he possessed urging otherwise, he knew he could not avoid what was, clearly, his fate. "And how would you like to spend this time?"

"In...education." She chose her words carefully. "You, if you'll forgive me for being bold, would seem to possess knowledge I should like to acquire."

"And you're quite sure none of those other fellows will do?" He gestured vaguely to the floors above them, where various of his more solvent peers still presumably paraded about.

"The bags of pants, you said?" Her look became skeptical. "I suppose Colonel Crathie *might* be persuaded—"

He could not let her even contemplate the thought. "That tired old war horse," was the kindest, most gentlemanly thing he could say.

"Just so," she agreed. "So, no, none of them will do. Because they seem to lack something you have." She leveled him with her forthright, solemn gaze. "Something I can't quite name."

He could name it. Because he had felt it too, from the very first time he had seen her, this near magnetic attraction. This craving for her presence. This want.

"Something I felt the moment you spoke to us this evening," she continued. "A sort of surprising recklessness."

Damn his eyes, yes. Reckless was exactly the right word. It was reckless in the extreme to let himself hope. And damn near insubordinate, to flout Augusta Ivers's direct orders.

Not to mention bloody dangerous to his heart.

"You've felt this way before, then?" He had to remind himself that however long he had worshiped her from afar, he didn't really *know* her.

"Perhaps," she admitted. "But not so…strongly or deeply. Or instantly."

He didn't know whether to be elated or leery. "And, if you will forgive my impertinence—I assume you've been kissed?"

She did not give way to embarrassment, though her cheeks pinked hotly. "Do you think me a practiced sort of flirt, Captain Balfour, because I have come away with you like this?"

"Oh, yes," he said easily enough, "because you were right—we *were* flirting. Quite delightfully. I enjoyed it. Very much. And I should very much like it to continue."

"Good," she said on an exhalation. "As do I."

He took the opportunity to step near to her. Her eyes were astonishingly clear in the moonlight. "You are a wonderfully frank lass for someone who has never been kissed."

This time her response was more arch than embarrassed. "I didn't say that I had never been kissed. I was out in London before we came here, Captain. Certain experiences practically come advertised with a girl's first season. Some kissing was inevitable."

"I imagine it was," he agreed graciously. "Entirely inevitable for a lass so beautiful as you."

The look she gave him was leveling. *"You've* kissed and been kissed, I assume?" she asked, keeping him on an honest, even keel.

"Aye," he answered truthfully. "Once or twice. Not as much as I'd like."

That made her smile. "Really?"

"I'm a navy man, lass, away at sea for years. There was no one I wanted to kiss on my ships."

She laughed, just as he had hoped, and it was everything for him to stand still and enjoy the happy sound without catching her up in his arms and whirling them both around until they were drunk on the simple pleasure of indulging in their attraction. "Just so. Some experiences come with the job."

He liked this pride, this certain confidence in her own experience. There was nothing missish about her. "I think, my very dear Miss Conway, that you have simply not been kissed by the right man."

She pressed her lips between her teeth, before she asked, "And are you—or are you willing to be—the right man, Captain?"

Was he? Against Lady Ivers's direct advice? Against all codes of gentlemanly conduct? Against his own better judgment?

"Aye, my dear Miss Conway. I most certainly am."

CHAPTER 7

"*P*lease." Flora sought to be herself even as her pulse began to thrum in her veins. "I pray you would call me Flora whilst you are seducing me."

It seemed the logical precursor to intimacy, this acknowledgment of each other.

"Flora." He breathed out her name as if it were perfume. "My dear, sweet, insightful Flora, I have not yet begun to seduce you."

She would have disagreed—the sound of her name upon his lips had already sent interesting little shimmers of sensation down her spine—but he reached one of his long, tanned, articulate fingers to brush a stray lock of hair out of her eyes, and something else within her fell to its metaphorical knees.

"This talk, this exploration of understanding," he said

with that intense, low, quiet voice, "is but flirtation—a prelude to seduction."

His words set a warm sort of vibration through her. She felt caressed even though he had only fleetingly touched her hair. "It feels like something more than mere flirtation."

"It ought to," he agreed with a slow, spreading smile. "Because what you are experiencing, my dear Flora, is the interesting thing known as *attraction*. Which ought always be the precursor to seduction. Which itself is the great instigator of *passion*."

"Ah." This time, she could hear the satisfaction in her exhalation. And feel the pleasure that glided like quicksilver along the surface of her skin. "I begin to see."

"Do you?" He reached for her hand, taking it between his before he turned their palms up, tracing the fingers of his other hand back and forth along her suddenly sensitive skin. "But before we can progress from attraction and flirtation to seduction and passion, we must first have understanding—of how far down the road of seduction you would like to travel?"

She allowed herself only the barest time to think— the time for thinking had been over the moment she had decided to bring him to the dark conservatory. "As far as this attraction will take me—or rather, will take us, I suppose."

"I suspect it might take us on a very long journey—if

we let it," he admitted. "Are you quite sure, sweet Flora, we shouldn't steer a safer course closer to the shore? That we shouldn't moor up in a quiet cove before we set sail for open water?"

After so many months being careful, of waiting as patiently as she might for something to happen—for Maisie or her father to make their decisions—she wanted nothing more than to take her own fate into her hands. "You think I will regret being seduced by you?"

"Yes," he said frankly. "When I am gone, back to some ship, in whichever war, in whatever part of the world, I think you may learn to think better of such a dangerous choice."

Flora was not so headstrong or stubborn as to immediately dismiss his advice. He was an experienced man of the world—it was, she innately understood, what attracted him to her. "Why is it dangerous?"

"Because, my dear Flora, I suspect we will like it—very much." His fingers traced a path of delight across the delicate skin of her wrist. "And you are *not for me*."

She forced herself to open her eyes that suddenly felt heavy and sanded with sleep. "And what is so dangerous about that? It sounds rather more lucky to me than dangerous."

"If our liaison were known, some people—" Narrow-minded, interfering, inconveniently rich people. "—would consider you ruined."

"Would you? Consider me ruined?"

"Nay, lass," he swore. "But I am not a man who would be a husband."

"And I am not a woman who would be a wife," she avowed. "Frankly, it seems a fool's errand, this forced march toward the altar. I want something more. *I* want to choose." She decided to be more candid. "And I should like to choose—however temporarily—you."

That he was both surprised and pleased by her declaration was evidenced by that wonderfully slow, spreading smile. "Well, then. Shall we see what it is that lies between us? There really is only one way to find out."

"One?" Even as his words sent a thrill skating across her skin, Flora could not help being herself. "I can think of at least three ways."

Oh, he liked that. "Clever, clever lass." He lifted her hand to press a kiss to her knuckles and Flora felt the sensation all the way from her fingertips down to her suddenly fluttering stomach.

He was so close. So close she could see the faint sketch of whiskers under his close-shaven skin. Close enough to catch the scent of citrus and far-away island spices. Her eyes closed of their own accord so she might go there, across the sea to meet him.

But he was here, with her, in this cold room that no longer seemed so chill. Looking down at her with warm intent. And she wanted nothing more than to meet that intent with her own. "Kiss me."

"Patience," he all but whispered against her skin. "No need to rush. We have all the time we might nee—"

Flora kissed him. She gave into the impulse and drew him closer, clasping his worn but impeccably tailored lapels. And then she held herself still, offering herself to him. Waiting. As patiently as she could.

He finally angled his head to kiss the corner of her mouth—a light, feathery little kiss that progressed along the seam of her lips. A kiss that was lovely, but at the same time disappointing.

"Jack." She wanted…something more. More than mere kissing.

"Aye?" he queried against a surprisingly sensitive spot beneath her ear. "Is something not to your liking?"

She did not want to criticize, especially while his lips pressed so pleasantly against her neck. It gave rise to an entirely new sort of sensation. Flora found her head turning away, offering herself up to the delicate delight that began to bud along the surface of her skin. She found her breath coming shallower and found she had opened her mouth slightly—a little silent "oh" of surprise and delight.

"Aye," he encouraged. He kept up his delicate play, moving his mouth along the line of her jaw, feathering pleasure along her skin until finally—finally—his lips settled upon hers.

Flora felt something akin to peace settle through her —that is, if peace were a buoyant, liquid thing that carried her up and away. That made her heart soar and her pulse thrum in her ears.

Jack Balfour kissed the way he seemed to do everything—with an easy competence and experienced command. Everything gracefully masculine. Everything sure and effortlessly controlled.

She felt her inexperience acutely and instantly—she who had thought herself so fully in control, pulling him down to her. But the moment his lips had firmed upon hers, she simply gave way to the heady, near intoxicating pleasure of his kiss.

Oh, yes, indeed. She liked this man. She liked this.

His clever, careful hands slid along the line of her jaw, urging her to turn ever so slightly more, to arch her head up to give him access. So his mouth and lips could delve deeper.

And then his arms came steadily around her, sliding to rest at the small of her back, while his mouth—his clever, sardonic, somehow smiling mouth—was doing impossible things to hers. Making her feel old and new and easy and fraught with delight, all at the same time.

He tasted of dark whisky and warm sunshine. He

smelled of starch and surety. Of exotic spices and the comfort of home. Of impossible possibilities.

For the first time in forever, Flora felt entirely, gloriously alive.

Again, and again his lips played against hers, tasting and exploring until she was doing the same. Until it was she who somehow needed to tangle her tongue with his and insinuate herself into his mouth. Into his warmth and wonder.

She brought her hands to cradle his face, to hold him as he was holding her. To take pleasure in feeling his smooth-shaven skin beneath her hands. In the glorious give and take of pleasures. He was all around her, his arms encircling her back, holding her gently, as carefully as if she were a precious thing.

But she was not precious and certainly not a thing—she was a woman who wanted control over her own life. Who wanted kisses and comfort. Wanted passion and peril.

And roguish, skeptical, secretly romantic Captain Jack Balfour *was* exactly the right man to give her both.

CHAPTER 8

*J*ack succumbed to the exhilarating intoxication of her. His eyes slid shut and he inhaled her essence—of spring blossoms and summer sun. Of lazy mornings and endless afternoons. Of sweet, soft—

At that moment, fate, or destiny, or simple ill-luck intervened—the door at the far end of the room rattled on its hinges.

Flora practically jumped out of his arms.

"I locked it," he assured her, just as the sound of a key being inserted into that very lock gave lie to his assertion. "Damn my eyes. We'll have to—"

"—hide," she finished, but she was already pulling him after her, retreating into the enveloping cocoon of the verdant ferns and palms at the farthest end of the glasshouse, plunging them deep into the velvet green dark.

And just in time.

"How strange that the room should be locked," a woman's voice penetrated their hiding place. "Though it's thankfully empty. And blessedly quiet. What a crush."

"Perhaps your aunt wanted to keep the conservatory private tonight," came a man's voice that Jack now reckoned must belong to Hamish Cathcart, who was husband to Lady Ivers's niece, the author Elspeth Otis Cathcart. Hamish was a younger son of the Earl Cathcart and a publisher of some note in Edinburgh. "I for one, think it a marvelous idea."

"Do you?" his wife queried absently. "Why ever—?"

Her question was answered by a low laugh, followed by the sound of the lock being turned over at the door. Though they were ostensibly hidden in the foliage, Jack instinctively turned his back to the room, wrapping Flora in his arms and urging her more protectively toward his chest.

"Hamish." The name held a playful warning. "Be good and let me light the lamp. I want to talk to you seriously about the manuscript I've been slaving over—"

"You shouldn't have to slave, my darling. Your publisher must be a brute to make you do so."

"Oh, he doesn't *make* me," the women's voice assured him playfully. "I want to. To please him."

"Methinks he should be the one pleasing you, lass," was the answer, which was swiftly followed by the soft sounds of lips meeting in passionate embrace.

After a brief, but not quite silent interval, during which the lamp remained unlit, Jack heard Mrs. Cathcart's breathy reply. "Oh, he does please me."

"Perhaps, he might please you more?" Cathcart queried.

"Hamish? What are you—" Whatever question the young Mrs. Cathcart might have posed, seemed destined to go unanswered—at least with words. "Oooh. Oh, yes, Hamish. Yes, please."

What followed, to Jack's acute ears, was the unmistakable sound of Mrs. Cathcart sinking onto the Admiral's comfortable chaise not more than ten feet from where he and Flora Conway stood hidden and being thoroughly and quite completely pleasured by her clearly devoted husband. Soft sighs and low moans permeated the thin barrier of the foliage until the air in their little cocoon of green began to grow as hot and humid as any summer's night.

Jack felt the moment Flora Conway realized exactly what it was she was hearing—he heard her faint gasp and felt her instinctive tensing as she shifted against him. He might have cautioned her by laying a hand across her no-doubt gaping mouth, but he dared not move at all—for a number of different reasons, the chief being his own instinctive physical reaction to both the stimulating sound of a woman being pleasured by cunnilingus and the softer sound of another woman's agitated breathing.

He held himself vigilantly still—squashed up as tight as they were, face to face, or rather, face to chest—lest she feel his inadvertent but persistent arousal.

But what was a man to do when the sounds of a woman being deeply pleasured filled his ears? With every moan and sigh, Jack's imagination was stretched tighter and tauter until he felt himself pulled as stiff as a backstay.

And if the uncomfortable shifting in front of him was any indication, Flora Conway was not faring much better. Her breathing changed, becoming shorter and less measured—she was so close, he could feel the rise and fall of her breasts above the taut boning of her stays.

"Easy," he whispered to reassure her, even though he risked their discovery.

Thankfully, the Cathcarts seemed to be too distracted for discovery.

Which was good, because once Jack had broken his silence, the urge to take up where he had left off gripped him stronger than ever. The urge to find her lips and put an end to this infernal hunger that had somehow devoured him whole. This need to be with her and for her.

He could not wait to taste her lips beneath his again. To find out how those soft breasts pressed against his chest might feel without all the intervening layers of clothing. Or explore the way her naked skin might feel stretched out atop his.

But he had to go slowly, stealthily, quietly. He had to fight to control his own breathing, because the air was beginning to saw in and out of his chest as if he had sprinted up the ratlines of a main mast, even with his two feet all but nailed to the ground.

And his torture had only just begun. Because in the next moment, Flora's hand landed tentatively on his hip —the barest weight, but he felt it echo through him like a cannon shot.

Yet, he did nothing. Well, nothing more than holding her a bit closer, perhaps.

For her own protection. And his own peace of mind.

Thus, tacitly encouraged, she moved her hand up along the taut column of his spine to the flat of his shoulder blade—a small, subtle pressure, yet he still felt as poleaxed as if she had run him through.

And then a slightly greater weight settled upon his chest—her head as she laid it against his lapels. She sighed, a silent exhalation of comfort and relief, but it was his eyes that fell closed as if of their own accord. As if the febrile weight of her was too much.

Or not enough. Never enough.

No, no, he was wrong. The feel of her in his arms, no matter the circumstance, no matter the embarrassingly erotic environment, was more than enough. It was perfect. He would impress this moment in his mind and heart and soul and make it last forever, a memory he would live on for the rest of his lonely life, in whatever corner of the globe fate took him.

But in that quiet moment, it seemed Flora Conway had decided to take fate, and something far more tangible, into her own hands. She wrapped both of her arms around him, hugging him closer, spreading her small palms wide across his back, testing out the length and breadth of him before she changed tack and found the way beneath the hem of his coat jacket, until there was nothing but the thin layer of his worn linen shirt between her hands and his skin.

His own hands nearly pulsed with the need to feel so close to her.

But before he could put thought into action, a cry came from Elspeth Cathcart. "Hamish!"

"My darling lass," her husband answered.

"Yes," was his wife's barely audible direction. "There. Yes. Please."

And judging by the immediate cries of bliss that

escaped the woman's mouth, her husband had done as charged, and done it very well indeed.

But all Jack could imagine as he shut his eyes tight was that it was the woman pressing herself against him making those sounds. And that it was he who was touching her and bringing her to such unmitigated bliss. That it was his mouth on her pale exquisite flesh. His fingers on her pink, ruched breasts.

Would she call his name? Would he call her his darling lass? What would she look like, all pale and flushed and spread out before him, her pristine white skirts pushed up, her soft, sweet belly, rising and falling with each excited breath. What would she taste like when he put his mouth to her flesh? What would she sound like while he brought her to the peak of her bliss?

The hell of it was, he would never know. What he could so vividly imagine, could never be. Because he was poor, and she was not for him.

But then, the divine Miss Flora Conway did something he could never have predicted—not in a hundred or a million or a hundred million years.

She sighed against him and then unerringly wrapped her hand around his cock.

CHAPTER 9

*F*lora made her choice.

She threw all caution to the wind and let her desires lead her where they would. And where they led was beneath the waistband of his breeches. To his member. His cock, undoubtedly. Jack Balfour seemed the sort of man who would say cock—blunt and straightforward, and yet still erotic.

He hissed in a sharp breath. "Flora."

"There," she encouraged on the barest whisper. "Was that so hard?"

He nearly laughed but stifled his exclamation into a silent huff of humor. "Yes," he returned low against her ear. "Infinitely so. Especially with your clever hand making me *hard*."

Yet despite this protest, he clearly liked it—he flexed his hips ever so subtly into the press of her hand. And so, without any further ado, she used her other hand to loosen the buttons of his fall front breeches. Slowly, deliberately, so he could stop her if he wished.

But he did not stop her, and in another moment, she delved into his breeches to take up the tender, hard length of him.

He inhaled another swift breath. "Two hands for beginners, I should think," he muttered.

It was her turn not to laugh. "Jack," was all she could manage. What a delight it was to flummox and please him all at the same time.

"Say it again." His voice was dark with whispered need.

But she didn't—not just yet. Not when she had him in hand. Not when his flesh was somehow smooth and astonishingly stiff all at the same time. And certainly not until he sucked in a long breath as she wrapped her second hand around the bare heat of him. "Jack."

"Oh, lass."

"Flora," she whispered. "Do you like that?"

"God's balls. Yes. Please, Flora." He took hold of her shoulders. "Are you trying to kill me?"

"Only a little," she admitted. "Is that not what the French call it, *le petit mort*, the little death?" She liked this heady admixture of attraction and wit and flirtation and erotic pleasure.

"The little death is for women," he gritted.

"I don't see why we shouldn't share."

He could not stop his laugh from echoing out into the glasshouse, and they both froze for a long moment, fearing for their discovery. But there was no other sound, no answering challenge.

Jack peered cautiously over his shoulder, through the foliage. "Thankfully, it seems that we are once again alone, lass."

"Flora," she repeated. "It seems only right to speak intimately while I'm grasping your person, Jack. Did they lock the door behind them?"

"You *are* killing me," he sighed. "But if you will be so kind as to let go of my cock, I will endeavor to find out."

"If I must," she agreed, doing as he asked by buttoning up his breeches.

"Thank you." He checked the buttons himself, straightened his coat and cuffs, and made his way across to the door, whereupon he threw the bolt. "Damn my eyes," he said with some relief. "Where were we?"

"Very pleasantly engaged." She shared his relief. "Gracious, but that was…educational."

His smile turned roguish as he came back to her. "And what did you learn?"

Flora decided that the slightly teasing but straightforward approach worked best with Jack Balfour. "That you like it when I hold your *cock*."

He did not demure. "Very much so."

"And whoever that was—no, don't tell me!" Flora held up a hand. "I should never be able to look them in the eye again or make pleasant conversation at a party. I shall be attempting to banish their names from my mind from this moment onward."

"As you should do with my name once we part."

"I don't think so," she countered. "I think I won't mind looking you in the eye, for the remembrance of your—"

"Don't say it."

"Cock," she mouthed silently, "will always give me great pleasure."

"My dear—"

"Flora."

"Flora," he finished. "I do feel compelled to tell you that I am more than capable of giving you something far more memorable than that."

"I am delighted to hear that, Jack, because that was the other part of that very educational interlude that I found curious."

"Aye?"

"Aye," she confirmed before she firmed her courage. "I think I should very much like to have whatever that was—" She made a vague gesture to indicate the goings-on on the chaise. "—done to me."

He grew instantly still in the way of a man with a loaded weapon. "Be careful what you ask for, Flora."

Again, she was no green girl to be instantly rejecting and rebutting his words. She felt, instinctively, that if she was going to choose this, *he* was the man to choose it with. "I promise you, Jack, I have spent the whole of my admittedly short life being excessively careful. Being diligently prudent. And I have been left entirely unsatisfied with prudence and caution." She looked up at him, so near but not yet near enough. "I should very much like to be if not exactly reckless, then sensibly indiscreet. With you," she added for clarity. "And your rather marvelous—" She dropped her glance in the general direction of his nether regions.

She did not get to finish, because suddenly he was there, his hands cupping her face, drawing her mouth up to his. Covering her lips with his. Pressing her back onto the chaise with the welcome weight of his body.

Everything within her ached and sighed with pleasure all at the same time.

"—your marvelous mouth," she finally finished.

He broke off from their kiss for a ruthless moment. "Not another word."

And then his leg insinuated itself between hers at the same time that she felt his hand at her thigh, fisting up the long fall of her skirt, drawing it ever higher until she felt the cool air on the skin exposed above her garter. And then his hand—that lovely articulate hand—was stroking the inside of her thigh, following the line of her leg up until—

His mouth covered hers, swallowing the sound of her astonishment. And pleasure.

He touched her again, fingering her flesh gently but purposefully. Oh, so purposefully, creating such sensations that she all but mewed into his mouth.

This man whom she had only just truly met that evening, whom she had only planned to tease and make like her. This handsome, outrageously attractive, witty, poor, penniless man who had his fingers inside her and was giving her exquisite bliss.

And he knew it. "Shhhhh," he breathed into her ear the very moment she felt a moan coming on. "Not a word. We don't want anyone to hear *us*." He kissed the hollow behind her ear, and she found herself turning her head to grant him greater access.

"I take that back," he whispered. "The only word—" He paused to place a kiss on the corner of her eye. "—is stop. If we do anything—if I touch you in a place you don't like, or in a way you don't like—you have only to say, 'stop.' What I do, I do for you, so if you don't like, you tell me. Aye?"

"Yes."

All the while he was whispering his instruction, his other hand had been gliding across the skin above her bodice, and she felt herself all but arching her back into the phantom weight of his palm. Hoping he would do exactly as he did, delving his fingers into the valley between her breasts to find the drawstring to her bodice.

He loosened her bodice, pushing the fabric aside, running his fingertips across the rounded swell of her breasts above the confines of her stays. And then he scooped his fingers into the soft cup of her stays to find and tweak her tight, aching nipples.

Her head fell back on a silent gasp and in another moment his mouth covered hers, kissing away her moan with his lips and clever tongue. He pushed her bodice lower, so it gaped across her chest, sliding her sleeves off her shoulders so her upper arms were trapped snug by her side.

And then, with one hand cradling her nape, and the other hand cupping her mound, he lowered his mouth to suck hard upon her nipple. And everything within her, every feeling and emotion came together to create a need so fierce and powerful it took away all thought all reasons. All of her senses became one—she could only feel.

Feel want. Feel need. Feel pleasure.

Within her, his fingers set up a gentle, steady rhythm, playing and caressing until it was almost too much—too much pleasure and need and aching incandescent joy—and not enough, all at the same time. She pushed up into the weight of his hand, so the pressure and pleasure became one and the same. So the rush of heat and desire began to bloom from within her belly and spread to the very edges of her being.

Flora opened her eyes to look at him in the velvet dark, this beautiful man looming above her. This thoughtful man touching and playing and murmuring incoherent words of passion and encouragement. Her body seemed to be winding itself around his hand, coiling higher and higher, closer to some unseen joy. Some not-so-distant meeting of mind and body and soul and pleasure so beautiful she wanted to laugh and cry all at the same time.

And so, she did. She laughed out his name while tears streamed down her cheeks. She smiled and gasped and smiled and cried until she could do nothing more.

The edges of her vision went dim, and she screwed her eyes shut tight and heat and joy and honeyed fire burst within her, and she was for the first time in her life, perfectly and incandescently exhausted. And happy.

So very, very happy.

CHAPTER 10

*J*ack gave himself the gift of an eternal minute to watch and listen to Flora slowly coming back to herself. To impress upon his memory what she looked like, all pale and flushed and spread out before him, her pristine white skirts pushed up, her soft, sweet belly, rising and falling with each slowing breath. To remember what she tasted like when he put his mouth to her exquisite flesh. To marvel at the sounds she made while he brought her to the peak of her bliss.

"Well." She let out a breath of laughing wonder. "Happy Saint Nicholas Day to me."

"I hope ours was a suitable celebration," he ventured with his own laugh, "to add to the others."

"Oh, gracious," she said on a mortified whisper when she finally met his eyes. "Was I as loud as *she* was?"

"My darling lass. Louder," he teased.

"Oh, Lord." A burst of pink re-blossomed on her cheeks before she covered them with her hands. "Gracious, Jack." She blew out a huff of disagreement. "You're meant to be kind and reassure me."

"Apologies, sweet Flora. But I'm not a reassuring sort of fellow." It was best she knew. "I'm too poor for platitudes." To lessen the stinging reintroduction of truth into what had up until that moment been a dream-like interlude, he added, "But we are quite alone, and I take the sounds of your delight as a sign of your approval."

Her relief was nearly as profound as her climax had been. "Thank God."

Jack wasn't quite ready to thank a deity he wasn't sure he believed in. But he sure as all hell believed in Flora Conway—now more than ever before. "I'd rather thank you."

"Oh." Her cheeks went that divine shade of sunset. "Thank *you*." She drew in a long breath before she added, "Thank you for the—" She seemed to be casting about for the right word.

"—climax? Orgasm?" he supplied. "Little death?"

"Do you know, it didn't feel like a little death—it felt more like a little life."

Her simple honesty was killing him. All he could think to say was, "This is why I like you."

She reached out to stroke his face. "Yes, what a backwards foundation for a friendship we've laid—lust and likability. What strange bedfellows."

"And we haven't been to bed, yet."

Flora managed to tip her head, even as she lay next to him. "I did not think we were aiming for a bed."

"No," he confirmed, much to his damn disappointment. "We are not. In fact, very shortly, what little bed I have will be but a canvas cot swaying from the ceiling beams. The comfort of ease is not in my future."

"We do not have a future," she said with that solemn insight of hers. "Except, I hope, in friendship. May I write to you on this bed-less, swaying ship of yours? As your friend?"

Something within him turned easy and regretful all at the same time. "Aye. I should like that. Now," he said a bit brusquely to cover his uncharacteristic descent into sentiment, "let us put you all to rights."

She blew out a breathy laugh. "I fear there's no chance of that, my dear Jack." But she was smiling as she stood on tottering legs to straighten her gown. "Gracious! My skirts are hopelessly crushed. My maid will have my head."

"For my own part, I would choose a different part of your anatomy to have, although, since your head is the place where the kissing happens, and is quite nice, I hope she will defer her wrath."

"Thank you, Jack. As is yours—your head. Quite nice."

"Damning each other with faint praise? That means it is time to go."

"Oh, no." She reached for his hand. "Please."

"No?" He was instantly back on his guard.

"No." She laced her fingers through his. "Not yet. I'm just feeling intolerably awkward thinking about facing the world again. I'm sure it will pass." A blush arose in her cheeks, but she held to her purpose. "If you will kiss me again. Please. Just once. Just once more, the way—"

He did not make her beg.

He kissed her. He put his hands on her shoulders and held her still and kissed her with every bit of lust and longing left within him. He kissed her with heat and fire and lips and tongue and desire that rose like a damn phoenix within, until he began to eye the divan with renewed purpose.

"Gracious," she said as she worked to regain her breath. "Most educational."

"And what have you learned this time?" he teased.

"That I am beginning to really, truly, and very sincerely, like you, too, Jack Balfour."

Another, even more unexpected hit—Jack felt shot clean through.

He tried through the years to give himself a character—to be a man other people might count on. To live up to his word when it mattered. To be amusing when called upon. He had felt himself a gentleman, a dutiful officer, a loyal friend, and a generous lover.

But until the moment Flora Conway had said she liked him, he had not truly understood the privilege, the true generosity of friendship. "I am honored."

"As am I," she rejoined easily. "And I am also glad. Though it seems little enough to say, again, thank you. This has been lovely."

His cynicism reasserted itself. "But?"

"No buts," she said with that solemnly serene smile of hers. "No conditions or recriminations. And certainly, no regrets."

This then, was her real gift—the gift of pleasure that had nothing to do with passion and everything to do with being content.

He had yet to learn to be content with what he had. Because it was impossible. Impossible not to want more. Not to want to bask in the warmth of her serenity for at least a little while longer. For as long as he could.

But she was already moving toward the door even as she offered him her hand. "I am sure we ought to return to the party."

He brought the small hand she had extended to his lips. "Yes, much to my regret."

"Come now—did we not just say no regrets?" she urged.

"You did. But I have lived too long in the world not to have some very real regrets, dear Flora. And I fear that the brevity of my association with you will very soon be added to that list."

"Brevity? Then you really must leave before Christmas?"

"I fear so," he confirmed. "I needs must make one more trip north to Kinloch to close up and shore up what is left of the house before I head for London. It is a three-day journey south to the capital, and despite Lady Ivers's prediction, not even the arrival of the savior at Christmastide will slow the mighty Admiralty from their purpose. Not this year anyway. With any luck, and enough money to raise and provision a decent crew, I should be into Portsmouth Roads before Epiphany."

"Though I have just found you, I am sorry to see you go."

"So am I." For the first time in ages, he actually meant it. He had trotted his removal out like a faithful dog trailing behind him, ready as an excuse to end any situation or conversation he found intolerable.

"Can I not convince you to stay for just a few days more?" she asked. "Would those few days really matter that much? Or even a few more hours?"

"I thought you said we should return to the party?"

"I did, didn't I?" She let out an exasperated sigh. "That would be the prudent thing to do. But the night *is* fairly young—it is just going on midnight. Perhaps we might continue our…discussion on the topic of education a little later on? After the supper?"

He made a show of consulting his watch. "I suppose I might spare a few more hours. Come, let me escort you upstairs." Jack offered her his arm.

"What if we're seen coming back together?"

"We will talk. We'll talk as if we've been having the most delightful, ridiculous, scandalous, ordinary conversation that we want to continue over supper, and we'll refuse to be interrupted by anyone. We will brazen it out."

CHAPTER 11

*F*lora had no real experience with brazen.

But she had never had any experience with being intimate with a man and look at how delightful that endeavor had turned out to be. She felt positively aglow with good feelings.

Christmastide was growing on her after all.

She linked her arm with Jack's and let the captain steer them where he would.

In another few moments, they reached the top of the stairway. Jack covered her forearm with his and bent his head low, as if they had been strolling along, wrapped up in the most intriguing conversation.

"Ready?" he asked. "Here is our useful fool, Colonel Crathie. Like this—" He raised his voice, so their conversation became audible. "No, no! That was back in the year ought, I'm sure. Let's ask, the colonel, here.

Crathie, my good man, wasn't that in the year ought? You'll remember, of course, the Corsican was up to his neck with revolts in the West Indies, was he not?"

"Certainly," was the colonel's staunch reply.

"Good man, Colonel." Jack patted him on the back. "And there you have it." And onward he led her, taking the whole time. "I was in *Excellent* at Cape Saint Vincent, you see, Miss Conway. Have you any great knowledge of that glorious battle? No? Well, you see—"

When at last they had made a full circuit of the drawing room, he lowered his voice. "And that is how you avoid the bores—by becoming one. Idiocy is a marvelous charm. People are afraid they'll catch it, so they move off as soon as possible."

"You really are incorrigible, Captain."

"Thank you. I do try."

"You succeed."

"Not yet," he muttered under his breath. "One more turn of the room should do it, Miss Conway," he advised. "Then you'll go get yourself your single glass of wine and—"

"My single glass of wine? How did you know that I—"

"—and if Lady Ivers is serving smuggled French wine," he went on quickly, as if he were determined to divert her attention from the fact that he seemed to know her habits too well. "Please be so kind as to not tell me. Take your supper with Lady Ivers—there is an empty seat next to her—and I will come and join you in good time."

"I will not inquire as to how she has maintained her cellar," Flora pledged with a smile. But it was another moment of education. How had she never thought where her glasses of wine came from? How had she never thought about how the hundreds of bottles her Papa had stored in the cellar at Kirk Brae Head might have arrived there during the years and years that the Royal Navy had been blockading Revolutionary, and now Napoleonic France?

She certainly thought about it now, as footmen circulated about the house, their trays laden with all manner of imported libations while she filled a plate from the laden table. Though her curiosity was high, she quietly slipped into her seat, and kept her musings to herself.

That was until Lady Ivers turned to her. "Good Lord, Flora, where have you been? No," the lady immediately contradicted, holding up her hand. "Don't answer that."

"I am right here," Flora attempted to follow Jack's direction to brazen it out, lying with a laugh. "Where else would I be?"

"Gone for an intolerable length of time," was the lady's pert answer.

Flora tried in vain to keep herself from blushing. "I must have…"

"Lost track of the time. Yes, certainly." Lady Ivers supplied the lie even as she shook her head. "You did right, coming to sit with me. It will make the talk die down."

"What talk?" Flora immediately looked around her.

"No, don't look," Lady Ivers contradicted. "And don't be obtuse. Did I not just tell you an hour and a half ago not to fall for the man? And what do you go and do— fall, clearly. You'll have to stay here, of course. We will make some excuse that you retired to your room to attend to a ripped hem. I'll have a footman take word up to Kirk Brae Head that you are staying here with me tonight, so that your own people will not worry."

"I don't think—"

"No, you didn't think, which is fine in its place, but that place is not my home. And that time was not tonight. I warned you!"

There was nothing Flora could say but, "Yes, my lady. I am sorry."

"Yes, well. Finish up your supper and then stay with me whilst I begin to see my guests—including a certain captain of the Royal Navy—off for the evening."

A word that might have been, "No," tried to escape her lips, but Lady Ivers's answering stare was unwavering. "Trust me to know what's best," the woman instructed, "though I daresay you like it not. But Rome wasn't conquered in a day—it took a steady campaign so that the day the barbarians arrived at the gates, they fell with ease. Not that you're a barbarian, Flora dear. Nor Jack either, but you take my point."

Flora did not, exactly, take her point. But what she did take was that it was again her turn for being told off. "Yes, my lady."

Lady Ivers finally nodded in satisfaction. "Good girl."

In another half hour, after the first of her ladyship's guests began to take their leaves, that lady summoned a footman. "Find Captain Balfour and bring him to me posthaste, there's a good man."

And when Jack dutifully appeared a few minutes later asking, "How can I be of service, my lady?" the lady was characteristically direct.

"You can do me the honor of taking the advice I, in my greater wisdom and infinite patience, have taken the time to give you, Jack. And you, Flora. She is *not* for you," Lady Ivers told Jack. "Spare yourselves the inevitable disappointment and torture of falling in love. It simply won't do. Now, take your leave like a gentleman before you make me regret this unfortunate need to give you a talking to." And then she belied her stern words by kissing him on the cheek and saying. "Content yourself with sending flowers and be done. I'll see you on Thursday next at Lady Cairn's, of course. Goodnight, Jack, darling. Off you go."

Jack donned his cynical hauteur along with his well-worn sea cloak. He was everything gentlemanly as he accepted Lady Ivers's directive as well as her embrace, making them an elegant leg before he raised her ladyship's hand for a kiss, though he used that moment to shoot Flora a look from under his furnished brows.

"I'm sorry," she mouthed wordlessly from behind Lady Ivers's back, both embarrassed and delighted to be doing something so school-girlish.

"An honor as always, my lady," Jack addressed to their hostess, before he turned to Flora with something like amused regret in his eyes. "Miss Conway, a very great pleasure to converse with you, however briefly. Good luck in your quest for purpose. I'm sure you'll find it."

It was exactly the right thing to say. "Thank you. And the same good luck to you, Captain."

"And I thank you." He jammed his battered tricorn on his head. "I'm going to need it."

"Yes," she said nonsensically, grasping for something, anything else to say. "I hope we will see you back in the city for Green Night," as Lady Cairn was calling her winter solstice celebration.

"Perhaps," was all he would commit to in Lady Ivers's presence.

And with that, he touched his hat and was away.

Flora watched him stride off, down the stairs and despite all her protestations of independence and no regrets, she could not but yearn to follow him. To see him in his own familiar surroundings. To find out every last shred of information about who he was when he was not roguishly propping up drawing room walls or bringing her to the peak of physical bliss.

The door closed behind him and Flora attempted to shake off the feeling of loss and call her good sense into order, only to find Lady Ivers regarding her through narrowed eyes.

"It is clearly even worse than I thought," the lady sighed. "Come along."

Orders were given and hasty preparations made and before Flora knew it, she was being ushered into a very pretty, silk-lined bed chamber, where quilts were being turned down on a very soft bed, and a fine linen sleeping shift was being warmed in front of the fire by a maid.

Lady Ivers fussed and clucked like a mother hen. "I hope you will be comfortable in here. This is Elspeth's room when she comes to stay."

Flora could not help the thought that materialized in her brain of the delights Elspeth might have experienced in the room—if the goings on in the conservatory were any indication of her amorous pursuits—though she endeavored to keep her embarrassment from her voice. "It is exceptionally lovely."

Lady Ivers dusted a nonexistent speck of dust off the silk coverlet. "Make yourself comfortable. If you need anything, you have but to ring for it." She gestured to the bell on the bedside table before going to the door. "I hope you sleep well."

"Thank you, my lady."

At the portal, the lady paused, as if in thought, before she turned. "And I hope, my dear, Flora, that he was worth it."

Flora, who had decided that trying to lie to Lady Ivers was a fool's errand, gave her the truth. "Most assuredly, my lady, he was."

"Good." The canny old woman's smile was as wide as it was sly. "I had very great hopes that he would be."

CHAPTER 12

*I*f Flora had expected some token from the captain, some small communication in the days that followed, she kept both her expectation and her subsequent disappointment to herself.

He did not send flowers.

He did not come to call.

He did not so much as send the merest note.

Despite her best intentions, Flora was taken aback. Surely, there would be some acknowledgement of their intimacy. Of their friendship? Surely, she did not have to go to him a-begging. Could she not expect such societal civilities of him?

Yet, she knew she was expecting too much. She knew their association was destined to be short lived, and she had accepted, even welcomed that fact. She had expressed no regrets.

And yet none of that kept her from missing him, this witty handsome man she had only met once. And none of it kept her from attending Lady Quince Cairn's Green Night Fête—"Calling it the Winter Solstice is far too witchy for current tastes," the lady had explained—in a state of near indecent anticipation.

Every one of her close acquaintances would be there, including her sister, Maisie, and her husband, Archie, who was a great friend of the Marquess of Cairn. Flora could only hope that the most important person, and newest of her acquaintances, would be there, also.

The evening dawned—if evenings could dawn, she supposed—inauspiciously. Freezing rain sleeted down upon the city at an almost horizontal angle, as if all the winds of the North Sea were being driven inland by a whip hand.

But these resilient Scots were making merry despite the filthy weather. The party at the Marchioness of Cairn's lovely townhouse on Charlotte Square was to begin at sunset, and Flora arrived at the appointed hour with Maisie and Archie in their carriage to protect her—and her best evening gown—from the raw elements, though the Cairn's residence was but a stone's throw from the Conway house at Kirk Brae Head.

And while outside was everything chill and inhospitable, within was everything warm and gay and inviting. The marchioness had festooned her home with every possible sort of greenery—laurel, bay, fir, holly, and ivy hung in fragrant swags above every doorway. But the center of Lady Quince's festive decorations was the 'kissing bough,' a sphere wrapped with ivy, holly and mistletoe, and adorned with red apples, oranges, spices, ribbons and candles.

Flora could only hope that Captain Balfour would appear to help her make good use of it. And also hope that her hopes for the captain didn't show on her face.

"What a delight to have you here this evening!" the Marchioness of Cairn greeted them. "I have not seen you out and about much this Christmas Season, Maisie. Nor you, dear Flora. You both look marvelous—that gown is enchantingly becoming."

"You are too kind, my lady," Flora allowed.

"I have been keeping rather close to home this season," Maisie answered. "And you know I'm not one for socializing."

"Perhaps," was all the Marchioness would allow. "But Flora has not your excuse."

"My apologies," Flora said simply. No need to reveal that she had been pining in private rather than in public these last few days.

The marchioness narrowed her gaze. "Do I detect a hint of melancholy?"

"Not at all," Flora lied through her smile. "Well, perhaps a bit, with my father—" She hated to trot out her poor papa's disgrace and self-exile, but it was hardly a secret, and far better to mention her father than the real reason she might—might—be melancholic.

How could she bring up his name? Who else were his intimate friends? How could she ask after him without giving herself away? What would Maisie think of her if she inquired after him? Who else could she ask?

Fortunately, she did not have long to wait. She knew the moment he entered the room—some internal barometer sensed the change in pressure. She counseled herself to be calm. She counseled herself not to blush, or worse, look expectant. Not to rush to him.

She would be happy, certainly, to see him. She would be warm and witty. She would make him laugh.

She cast a calm smile his way while he made his good evenings to the Marchioness of Cairn, but kept her attention on Maisie and Greer, the Duchess of Crief and her husband, the Duke.

"That sounds quite lovely, Your Grace. I have never been to the Highlands, myself," Flora prattled. "The city of Edinburgh has been study enough for me this past year."

Flora hoped she wasn't talking absolute nonsense, as she smiled and nodded and tried to keep her attention on the people in front of her. Despite the fact that the duke and duchess excused themselves to greet Jack a short while later, Flora made herself take stock of the time and take a deep breath before she allowed herself to wander away from Maisie and join their group, as if she had all the time in the world and was not there expressly and exclusively to see and speak to him.

"Captain Balfour, good evening." She tried to suppress her joy into warm civility.

Jack made a perfunctory bow to the whole of their small group before he flicked the barest glance her way. And only when it was either overlook her or be rude, did he deign to add, "Miss Conway."

She thought she saw him swallow, as if taking a bitter dose of medicine, but her concern was swept away by his coldness. He was as standoffish and chilly as if they had never met. As if he had no desire to even remember her.

Confusion was like a damp fog creeping upon her. But she would not dissemble. She would not be embarrassed.

"Are we not friends, Captain Balfour?" She finally managed after Lady Creif had somehow herded her husband away. "Are you not happy to see me?"

"My dear Miss Conway. I fear not." His step away was jerky, not at all his usual gracefully masculine self. "I may not allow myself the pleasure. I dare not." He made another, almost terse bow and would have withdrawn from her, had she not stopped him.

"Come now, Captain," she tried to echo the teasing

charm of their last meeting. "You know it won't do. We are under the kissing bough."

He immediately stepped back. "It will have to do, Miss Conway." His voice was without warmth. Without pity. He made another curt bow. "Please. I am leaving." He tugged at the cuff of his coat in a gesture of impatience. "On the morrow. The Admiralty have indeed chosen me and bid me come. Immediately. A ship awaits in Portsmouth. I must be gone. I came only to make my farewells to friends to whom I owe..."

The brief look he gave her was nothing but agony. All that rage and grief she had sensed in him was, for one awful moment, laid bare.

"I'm so sorry," was all she could manage.

"Forgive me, I beg you." His voice was as frayed as an old rope. "But I must bid you goodbye." And, without looking at her again, he took his leave.

Misery cut into her like a raw wind out of the Highlands. She could barely breathe. She did not think she could even move from where she stood, frozen upon the floor.

But Flora forced herself to move, and then after a few hesitant steps in one direction, and then another, found that she *needed* to move. To give her something to do instead of dissolving into tears. To exercise the corrosive feeling of failure that tasted like acid in her mouth.

But in her heedless flight she found herself at the vestibule of the front door, where Jack was taking his leave of the marquess.

"Godspeed, Jack," Alasdair, Marquess of Cairn was saying.

"Cairn," was all Jack said as he shook the marquess's hand and, without so much as a single backward, rueful glance at her, fled into the sleety night.

"I wonder what we said to scare him off?" Lady Cairn murmured, appearing silently at Flora's side. "Not a whit of wit out of him tonight, did you notice?"

"I did." Flora all but stammered her reply. But even she could hear the telltale aching regret in her voice. She strove to care less. "And Captain Balfour is renowned for his wit and amusing manners, is he not?"

"He is," Quince confirmed. "But if you ask me—and I know you did not, but I cannot help noticing such things—before this evening, I thought I detected an interest in *you* from him."

"Did you?" Flora felt her eyebrows might fly right off her face with surprise.

"I really did," the marchioness insisted. "And even this evening, he kept darting surreptitious looks at you the whole time he was here—which granted, was not long—when he thought no one was looking. But I was. I saw it."

"How...strange," Flora finally concluded. "He did not

speak to me above three or four words. And he clearly was not pleased with the company."

"Oh, you mustn't think that! He was clearly miserable with himself and his circumstances. I am sure he was entirely preoccupied by his imminent return to his profession—though it is a shame that such a man should have to return to the navy because the earldom cannot support him. Such gross mismanagement from his forebears, if you ask me."

"Yes," Flora agreed with just as much regret. "A vast deal of mismanagement."

"Too vast a deal," Lady Quince agreed. "That such a man should be so at the mercy of the winds of fate— quite literally, upon the seas!" she added for emphasis. "Well, it's just not right."

"No." Flora could do nothing but agree while she continued to fight back her tears.

But Quince, as the marchioness had repeatedly asked Flora to call her, was looking at her rather sympathetically, Flora thought, and she was far too miserable for subterfuge. "I wonder if I may ask you something in confidence, my lady?"

"Certainly." Quince was all assurance. "I am particularly good at keeping confidences, for I understand their import."

Flora damned her metaphorical torpedoes. "How well do you know Captain Balfour?"

"Jack? My husband knows him very well," Quince said quickly. "Thinks him an excellent fellow. Exceptionally brilliant captain." She took Flora's elbow and steered her to a less public spot so she might speak more confidentially. "What it is you particularly wish to know?"

"Your own opinion of his character, I suppose. For women often see things differently from men, like your esteemed husband."

"I find his character sterling, despite his reputation as a rogue," the marchioness answered immediately. "Unimpeachable. Loyal to a fault. Exemplary frigate captain the newspapers say, and Alasdair thinks they are the best of the navy, the frigate men. The heart of the service, he calls them. Charming and handsome, to boot. But you will have come to that conclusion on your own."

"Yes." He certainly was a handsome man. "If you like that weathered, seafaring type."

Quince's eyebrow arched in suspicion. "Did you not?"

Flora tried her best to dissemble. "I suppose."

"Yes, I think half of Edinburgh has been at least a little in love with Jack Balfour—his charm, not to mention his wit, is legendary."

It hurt to hear that his behavior to her had not been so out of the ordinary. But at the same time, it also helped. "He does give his charm quite freely."

"Has…?" Quince drew her back toward the wall where they were entirely private. "Has Jack somehow… trifled with your affections?"

"No, no," Flora insisted. "Certainly not trifled. But I thought we had…" She could not think of what to say that might not reveal and expose her. "Lady Ivers warned me that he is not to be considered—that he is poor."

"Yes, damn it. That's that fate I was railing against but a moment ago. But he is poor, poor man. So, what he needs is clearly a rich wife, though what he also needs is a sensible, independent woman, and I fear rich and sensible do not often come together in one person."

"No," Flora agreed. "It's all too sad."

"Yes, but are you leaving?" she asked, though it seemed to Flora that it was the Marchioness who was steering her toward the door. "Miss Conway's things, if you please," Lady Cairn called to the footman attending the portal. "But let me find you a good stout pair of mittens."

"You are very kind, my lady, but it is not so far to home that my hands will become that chilled."

"But what if you should find yourself wanting to make snowballs?"

"Snowballs?" Flora was entirely confused on top of being intolerably sad. "Why should I want to make—?

"To pelt upon someone's windows. From the rear

garden. A handful of pebbles will work in the summer, but a snowball upon a window—a first floor bedchamber window—should be a fun way to get someone's attention. The sort of someone who might have rooms on the mews behind King's Circus. Which can be accessed neatly from India Street, just a few blocks north." She tipped her head helpfully in the desired direction. "My intelligence tells me it's the second window from the right of the first floor of number twenty-six. Take a footman or a groom if you can. But the snow should keep the idle ill-doers away."

Flora was reduced to stammering again. "I thank you, my lady."

Quince pressed a quick kiss upon her reddened cheek. "Thank me when all is right between you and the gentleman in question."

"I will do." If she dared.

And was very, very lucky.

CHAPTER 13

lora did not go to him. Not immediately.

First, she needed a plan. And far more courage than she currently possessed.

And at least a dash of recklessness.

So, she weathered the short sedan chair ride home as patiently as she could, all the while debating and discarding different means to get to King's Circus.

She could not possibly go on foot in such weather, and certainly not in her evening clothes and slippers as thin as paper. And she would need to wake her last remaining groom in the stable to drive her. Although it wouldn't be the most outrageous request anyone had ever made of young Davie—Maisie had once all but stolen a pony cart from under the boy's nose—a trip for a potential tryst would be a first for Flora.

And to do any of this, she would have to get past Raines.

But if she did not go to him, or at least try, there was a very good chance that he would never be her lover in full. And that, she knew, she would regret until her dying day.

This was her chance. She would simply have to take Jack's advice and brazen it out.

"Come in, come in, miss." Raines greeted her at the door. "Out of this dirty weather, though at least it's turned to snow. We'll have a proper Christmastide." She immediately unfastened Flora's velvet evening cloak. "I hope you've had a pleasant evening?"

"I have not," Flora averred. "It was most unsatisfactory. But I have plans to make a reversal," she said as she headed up the stairs without waiting for the maid's reaction. "If you'll help me change into more suitable clothes, and fetch me a heavier cloak for this weather, and send word out to Davie in the stable to ready the small carriage." She dove into her armoire to take out a warmer, more practical gown. "I would appreciate it."

Raines stared at her. And at the gown she had chosen. "Where do you think you're going in *that*, if I may ask, miss? At this time o'night?"

"Please don't fuss," Flora all but pleaded. "I know what I'm doing." She had to go to him. She had to make sure he understood her regard.

She had to take this one small chance for happiness.

And if the encounter was to bring her unhappiness, better she know that as soon as possible, so she might get it over with. She could not be wondering about Jack Balfour and pining for him for years on end. It would never do.

"It doesn't matter what I'm wearing."

"As if," Cora Raines said half under her breath. "I can see you've got your heart set on what your heart wants to be doing, and there'll be no stopping you, so I'm not going to even try. But that gown may be practical for any old winter's night, miss, but it'll never do for bringing a gentleman up to snuff. Come you here and let me set you up proper." The maid very quickly chose a seldom worn, but beautiful gown of dark green velvet, that was cut a great deal lower across the bodice, exposing a vast deal more of her bosom than Flora normally liked.

"Clocked stockings, very fine. Half stays," Raines decreed as she turned about the room to find the listed items. "Less work coming off as well as on, and they'll set you up nicely. And your best shift. You've got a lovely bosom if you'd only show it off. No sense in not doing you up proper." She had Flora's first ensemble off, and the nearly transparent lawn shift out and over Flora's head before the latter could argue.

And why should she argue—Raines was undoubtedly

right, though the thought of getting down to her shift with Jack Balfour made her giddy and edgy all at the same time.

"There," Raines approved as she tugged the low bodice into place over the tight half-stays. "That'll do you nicely. Now let me loosen up your coiffure a bit—ever so slightly, so you look just that trifle undone, if you know what I mean, miss. And even if you don't, just trust your Raines. I know what I'm about. Got your sister that fine husband of hers despite her not caring a whit about what she threw on her back, now didn't I?"

"Did you?" Flora had not been aware of any efforts Raines might have made to bring Archie and Maisie to book, as it were.

"Made sure she always had beautiful shifts under all those dowdy smocks and shapeless round gowns. Made sure those fine lawn shifts showed, just that nice little bit, to catch Mr. Archie's eye, didn't I?"

Flora was astonished to find that anyone other than herself had been working to further Maisie and Archie's clandestine courtship. "I had no idea you were such an infernal genius, Raines. Thank you."

"You're welcome, miss." Raines took the compliment in her usual matter-of-fact way. "Now, let me pin this veil—don't you think about arguing with me, miss. You'll go veiled and hooded and as anonymous as a milkmaid if you know what's good for you."

"Yes, Raines." Flora didn't dare disagree—not when Raines was doing such a superb job.

"There's a good lass. There." The maid stood back to survey her handiwork. "Now, you go and give your fella a proper goodbye and do what you've got your heart set on doing. But don't you think of waiting until the sun is up to come home. You get yourself back here before the dawn if you know what's good for you."

"I do know what's good for me," Flora swore. "And I will do just as you say, Raines." She hugged the woman tight. "Thank you."

"You're welcome," the maid said as she shooed her charge toward the door. "Now off with you, before I change my mind."

Flora went.

The address Lady Cairn had given her was on the backside of the King Street Circus, where the smaller mews houses faced a hayfield above the village of Stockbridge.

She had Davie, her last remaining groom, who now acted as coachman, leave her at the top of the street, so the sound of the carriage might not attract any attention. Cleaving to Raines's warning, Flora made sure both her veil and her hood were well in place before she ventured down the length of the street, though the enveloping material did make it difficult to see—she had to lift the veil to be able to read the number twenty-six posted discreetly above his door.

But she let it down again to gather her courage in hand and take the brass knocker up before she let it fall.

The door was wrenched open immediately.

Jack was clearly not expecting her—or any visitors at this time of night—for he was clad for travel in his sea coat and boots when he answered the door with a single stubbed candlestick in his hand, scant illumination in the dim interior behind him.

"I hope I'm not intruding," she began in a rush, before she changed her mind. "On second thought, I hope I am intruding, for I should very much like to come in."

"Flora." He stood as still and staring as an owl. "Thank God. I was just coming to you. But here you are instead. You astonish me."

"No more than I do myself." She shifted from one cold foot to the other. "But I hope I do not astonish you so much that you do not invite me in."

"Yes, of course. By all means. Come, quickly now." He stood back to let her in before he stuck his head back out the portal into the snow, looking up and down the mews row.

"I'm sorry," she said. But the truth was, she was not sorry at all. "I had the carriage leave me off at the end of the row and drive on immediately," she explained. "He'll circle back to make sure I've gotten in but won't linger."

"Excellent. What a well-trained coachman you must have for midnight assignations."

Flora was determined not to take offense. "Thank you, but as this is our first assignation, we were unsure of how to get on. So, I'm glad you approve of our precautions. We very much wanted to get them right."

That finally brought a smile to his otherwise grim face. "You have, thank God. Well done, lass. I ought not be surprised by your keenness anymore. And I ought not look gift horses in the mouth."

"No, you should not," she agreed with some relief. "And although I am not, I hope you will agree, a horse, perhaps you may want to greet me by the mouth?"

"I do, lass. With pleasure."

He drew her into his embrace and slanted his mouth across hers, taking her lower lip between his teeth to worry at without biting. To lure her into the promise of more.

"Oh, yes, please," was her answer. "I knew I couldn't let you go without some word, some last gesture between us."

"My dearest Flora." He hugged her closer. "I was just on my way to you to do the same. To beg your forgiveness for my earlier behavior and to.…just beg."

"Jack." It was the only thing she had to offer, the gift of his name—the only thing other than herself. And so, she offered that too. "I came to ask your forgiveness for not understanding—" She suddenly found her tongue tied up on the lie. "No. I came to try and make love to you."

His smile dawned slowly but grew stronger with each passing moment. "Have you?" he queried with that delicious little half smile before he took her chin in his hand and turned up her mouth for a sweet, solemn kiss. "How charming of you." He took hold of her hand, his fingers interlacing with hers before he raised it to his mouth for a kiss. "If that is so, then you had best come with me."

He led her through a cold parlor where a number of sea trunks were stacked, ready for his imminent departure.

She had almost left it too late. Pride had almost robbed her of this pleasure.

Flora followed him up a narrow set of stairs to a spare but well-appointed bedroom, with a good armchair by the fire and a bed of no mean size, covered in well-laundered linens.

He had followed her gaze. "I may be poor," he quipped, "but I have standards. I also have firewood, still, so let me draw you close enough to warm you through."

"I rather hoped you might do that yourself," she said rather baldly. Who knew how much time she had with him—an hour or two at most? His mail coach would likely leave for London at dawn. She had wasted precious time prevaricating over society's strictures.

But he seemed to understand their urgency. "Then I will," he said, tossing his sea coat aside without ceremony. "Most thoroughly. But it is a raw night, and your hands are like ice. I will attend to warming them once I've built up the fire."

A glance at the basket next to the hearth revealed only a handful of logs left. Other than the bed, the room was laid nearly bare. She hated to think of him in such straits. "Please don't use up the last of your wood."

"I'll be gone on the morrow," he said reasonably while he laid the fuel on the low fire. "And I should far rather see you made warm in the perpetual winter of this city than leave the logs to crumble into dust waiting for me to return."

"Will it really be that long before you come back?"

"Years, if I'm lucky." He stood and returned his gaze to her. "Come, we must get you out of these wet things. Your toes must be as frozen as your fingers."

He drew her to the armchair and knelt beside her to untie and draw off her half-boots, taking her stocking-clad feet between his hands to chafe and warm.

Flora had never been more glad of Raines's thoughtful, practical preparations. Knowing she was clad in her finest gave her leave to think only about the way his hands kneading the soles of her feet made her feel—like a cat in a sunbeam, all hedonistic ease and delight. "That is…marvelous."

"I'm glad you think so, for there are more marvels to come," he said as he drew her stockings off and rose to hang them to dry on the fireplace screen.

Rather than wait for him to return to her, Flora rose with him, looped her arms around his neck and pressed herself against him, angling her mouth to his, offering him everything she was, body and soul.

She closed her eyes and let her lips find their own way, softly at first, learning the taste and feel of him, letting her passion grow of its own accord. Taking her own sweet time.

She kissed him gently, lightly, pressing little busses along the rough line of his jaw. Sipping him in until she was ready to drink her fill.

He opened his mouth to her, inviting her into taste and explore the clean winter taste of him, of whisky and rain. Her hands grasped at his linen shirt, holding him close and closer still so she could kiss him for as long as she pleased. Forever and a day.

"My divine Flora," was all he said. And all he needed to say.

All the restlessness bottled up inside her was uncorked and turned into daring, decisive action.

She pressed what she hoped was a persuasive kiss to the sensitive slide of skin below his ear. "My darling captain, won't you please make love to me?"

CHAPTER 14

"*L*ass." Jack seemed to need no persuading, because he smiled at her and took her face carefully between his hands. "You know I will do anything and everything within my power to make you happy."

"You already have." Gratitude, and something more, made Flora duck her eyes away from his, but her answer was a kiss to the hollow of his throat, where his pulse beat strong and steady beneath her lips.

He drew her mouth back up to his and kissed her—a kiss that soon turned searing enough to chase away the last lingering bittersweetness from the moment. From that point on, she knew nothing of regret and everything of want and need and the desire to learn more. To experience more.

"You're still in those wet clothes. If you'll allow me?"

He unerringly found the hidden drawstring on the bodice of her gown and tugged it free.

It was as if her skin came alive of its own volition where he touched her. Beneath the layers of her clothing, her breasts seemed to swell and become sensitized to even that fleeting contact. "Yes, certainly," she managed on nothing more than a whisper.

Jack came around behind her, tucked his chin against her shoulder, and murmured, "This gown, lass," as he loosened the neckline and brushed the fabric aside, running his hands down her bared shoulders. "Lovely." His mouth found a spot at the edge of her collarbone, and he pressed a warming kiss there before his teeth nipped gently at the sensitive sinew.

Flora felt her head turn aside as if granting him greater access. He could do whatever he wanted, as long as he did not stop.

His clever hands went to the back laces of her stays.

"Jack." It was a pleasure to say his name, to reach up and feel the now familiar contours of his face and stroke along the strong line of his jaw.

He turned his face into her hand, rubbing and scuffing his early beard against her palms, letting out a sound of near animal satisfaction in the simple pleasure —a pleasure she wanted, too. His hands on her skin, his lips on her body, his tongue tasting her.

She guided him to her mouth eagerly, pressing into

the kiss, hoping he could taste the desire on her lips the same way she could taste it on his. She was hungry for him.

And for no one else.

The bittersweet realization brought a pang of regret —an ache that she knew would grow in his absence— that she instantly banished.

She was with him now.

She would cherish him now.

He must have felt the same sense of urgency—his arms tightened around her, lifting her up and carrying her away to the bed, where they came down together in a lazy tangle of limbs. His leg insinuated itself between hers, riding intimately against her inner thigh. His tongue delved into her mouth while his hands roamed over her back, tugging her stays loose before hugging her close. He hands skimmed over her chemise before they raked through her hair, scattering her pins and cradling her skull so he could hold her still to kiss and kiss again.

"Yes." She gasped her encouragement. Heat began to pulse through her veins, driving away the last of the winter chill, warming her throughout. She surrendered herself to the comfortable pleasure, losing herself in the welcome force of each new sensation, until she wanted no barriers between them. No pretensions, no false modesty.

She shrugged herself out of her sleeves and tore away the loose stays so she could loosen the tie to her chemise and bare herself to his gaze.

Though her eyes threatened to sweep shut from the sheer tenderness of her emotions, she held them open, taking in the sight of him above her. Touching him, stroking his tanned face and his burnished hair and his strong neck.

But his clothing was barring the way to further access to his glorious person. "Now you."

Flora helped him along, pulling his linen shirttails free of his breeches while he obligingly shucked off his open waistcoat and peeled the linen shirt over his head, exposing his broad, bronzed chest for her. But even as her hands began to skim across the warm expanse of his skin, the weight of his body pressing down upon her just there—where his hips straddled hers—was so pleasing and soothing and exciting that her eyes slid closed just to be able to take in the exquisite pleasure.

Her clever brain was already figuring out how to get more of that pleasure—her hips seemed to rise to snug themselves into the delicious weight of him even as she reached to pull him down to her. She wrapped her arms around his strong shoulders and pulled the press of his body onto her.

"Flora," he breathed into her ear. "How I have wanted

you. How I have dreamed of this moment, with you beside me."

Flora's eyelids crashed shut at his tender touch, so sweet and gentle under the brittle armor of his cynicism. There was nothing cynical about him now, as he sent soft, slippery sensations skimming under the surface of her skin, seeping deep into her bones.

She let the divine tension pulse through her, coiling tight in the depths of her belly while he kissed and touched and stroked her way across her willing, welcoming body.

He lifted himself away from her and Flora heard herself moan the loss of him. But it was only for a moment, while he gathered the bunched skirts of her velvet gown and chemise and stripped them away, down the length of her legs.

For the barest moment she felt herself exposed and vulnerable, but even as one of his hands went to the buttons of his breeches, the other found the soft flat of her belly, pressing down ever so slightly with a sort of reassuring promise of different, less soothing pressures to come.

Flora surrendered herself to the exquisite pleasure of watching him look at her breasts, her body. She gave in to the bliss bursting across her skin when he lowered his mouth to take first one breast, and then the other into his mouth, the pull of his lips upon her sending arousal spiraling deep within.

His hand stayed put, his warm palm pressing into her belly, holding her still as he laved and nipped at her, encouraging her back to arch into the pleasure. "Yes," he urged on a whisper. "Show me what you like. What you need."

She closed her eyes and followed where her senses led her, stroking his shoulders, marveling at the shape and feel of him, inhaling the clean scent of him, tasting the salty warmth of his skin down the curve of his arm. "I only need you."

She opened her eyes when he levered himself off her, watching through her lashes as his hands trailed lower, across her belly to the vulnerable skin of her inner thighs, kneading her flesh until she was nothing but want and greedy need.

Flora opened her legs to him, and a soft rush of sensation made her gasp when he trailed the backs of his fingers through the curls at the juncture of her thighs. She felt her body grow taut and hot, as he parted her sex with his thumbs before he slipped his fingers inside her, touching her deeply, stroking powerfully and lightly at the same time.

Her body felt new and alive and warm and satisfied, but still not entirely satisfied at all. Satisfaction was a slippery tension that continued to elude her. The only constant was Jack.

She heard herself sigh at the wonder of it all, of him. At the skill with which he gave her pleasure with his hands and his tongue and his body as he settled his weight into her.

"My divine Flora," he murmured.

But he was wrong. She was not in the least divine— she was only human, with a human's need for the comfort of pleasure. With a woman's need for release. With her own unique need for him.

He eased his fingers from within her and carefully settled himself between her legs, stroking his hands down the naked length of her body until he gripped her gently by the hips. She could feel the sweet length of him pressing against her mound, and she found herself arching up into his warmth, into the reassurance of his body, into the promise of the pleasure.

And then he was pushing into her, filling her with his body and his passion and his desire.

A momentary discomfort came and swiftly went, carried away by the overwhelming feeling of satisfaction.

"Jack." His name was permission and plea.

"Flora." Her name sounded like a benediction from his lips. "Tell me you're fine."

Even in this moment, at the slippery edge of bliss she could not help but tease him. "Hadn't you ought to be telling me I'm *fine?*" She smiled and pulled his lips to hers for a kiss, too happy not to share her improbable, giddy joy.

"So fine," he assured her. "So very, very fine. The finest."

"Jack!" She laughed and somehow it made it better—happiness hummed through her like a drowsy bumble bee, all buzzy expectation.

And when he laughed with her, their shared joy became a physical thing, vibrating through her, heightening the rhythm of his movements as he pressed into her. She felt sated and happy and alive. His lips brushed against her ear, kissing and nipping and soothing as he whispered words of love and encouragement. "Sweet Flora. Yes. Damn my eyes, yes."

She held him to her with everything she had within her. With strength and determination, as if she could keep him with her always. And in that embrace, he rolled, carrying her atop him, propping her away from him so that she was seated firmly upon his clever, clever cock.

For a moment she could only regret the loss of him—of his warmth and weight—until new sensation began to spiral through her. New pressures that brought new ease, as well as new urgency.

He coaxed her shoulders back, filling his palms with

her breasts, tweaking and taunting her nipples, playing her as unerringly as a master. Making every part of her body feel connected to the next and the next until each pleasure coalesced into one single flame of need within.

Until she was the one pressing her weight into him.

Until she had to close her eyes to keep the heat and the light from blinding her.

Until heat blossomed over her like a wave, rippling all the way through her. Over and over and over again until everything within was perfect and exacting bliss.

And then he gripped her hips and surged up into her with a shout of wonder and thanks as he found his own release. "My God, Flora!"

"I'm here," she whispered as she collapsed down onto the exquisite bed of his chest. "I'm yours." And he was hers. No matter when he went, no matter how long he was gone, he was hers. He would always be hers now. Nothing could ever take that away.

CHAPTER 15

*J*ack came back to himself slowly—listening and feeling her breath even out against his chest. Keeping his arms wrapped around her as long as he could. Knowing the feeling of her in his arms, was everything he could have hoped. Was more than he had ever dared to dream.

He had found out how her soft breasts had felt pressed against his chest without all the intervening layers of clothing. He had explored the way her naked skin felt and looked stretched out atop him.

Like a fleeting glimpse of paradise.

He had the memory he would live on for the rest of his lonely life, in whatever corner of the globe fate took him. He waited until the last vestige of warmth had faded from the fire, and the chill of the night settled over their entwined bodies, hating that he could do nothing to make the moment last. "Come, my love," he said when he could find his voice. "Let me see you home."

"Must you?" She raised her head to look into his eyes. "And am I really your love?"

"You are my divine, exquisite, very fine lover," he told her. "As I am yours."

"Yes," she smiled, all drowsy, naked satisfaction. "Very fine." She reached to absently clasp his hand. "And while I might have expected that, I just never expected to like you so very, very much."

Her friendship was a finespun, delicate thing he would treasure. "Aye." He brought her hand to his lips to kiss. "Far better to be able to part as friends than merely sexual acquaintances."

"There's a cold phrase," she said in her remarkably straightforward way. "But must we really part so quickly?"

"My plans—the Admiralty's plans for me—cannot wait, I'm afraid. And since there are many things that we cannot choose"—he used her wording purposefully—"I can choose to try to protect you as I am able. And that means, getting you home where you belong."

"Yes," she finally agreed with him. "I knew this moment would come, but I still do not like it." Flora sat up and reached for her chemise to draw over her head.

He watched her lazily, still reclining on the bed,

begrudging the need for her to screen her body from his ardent gaze. "Do you need help with your stays? Your stockings. Anything?"

"Oh, certainly, if you would like to play maidservant. And I may play your valet."

"I fear if that were to happen, we would be here a great deal longer, and your presence might be noted."

"Yes, do good by stealth, the Bible says." She tossed him a delightfully playful wink, and he was struck again —a bullet right to the quick—by how much he *liked* her.

He laughed with her, but otherwise stayed where he was upon the bed, wanting to stay forever in this daydream of intimacy between them, this lovely interlude between what came before and what was to come after.

But his indolence could not last. And Flora was already donning her stays.

"Allow me," he said anew as he stepped behind her to lace her into the garment, dropping a kiss on the sweet curve of her neck when he finished.

She reached up to touch the spot as if she wanted to impress the feeling upon herself. "You make an admirable maid." She smiled as she teased, clearly trying to keep the mood light as they donned the clothing they had scattered here and there about the room in their haste to get them off.

"I live to serve," he reminded her in the same vein. "I

pray you will think of me whenever you are in need of lacing."

"My dear Captain," she said with her hand over her heart. "I fear I will think of you far more often than that."

He could not help but kiss her and taste the bitter-sweet tang of salt from the tears she was trying desperately to hide. "Come, no tears."

"No," she vowed, swiping them away with her sleeve. "I will be right as rain. I promise."

"Good lass." But he himself had to turn away to finish his dressing lest the hot sheen of tears have time to collect behind his own eyes. "I'll call us a hackney cab," he said as he shrugged on his greatcoat. "There's usually one or two idling in King's Circus."

"Oh, let us walk, please. I will be veiled and hooded and we can surely elude anyone who might recognize you if we take the way back across Stockbridge and down the path along the Leith Water to Queensferry Road. No one will see us there."

Once again, he was glad of her keenness of mind. "A sound path," he agreed, "but it will be fearsome cold at this hour of the night."

Flora looked to the small clock on his mantle ticking the hour close to four o'clock. "It will be fearsome cold in a cab without the warmth from the exercise of walking."

He surrendered to her will. "Aye, it will. So let us walk." He much preferred the privilege of being with her as long as possible. There would be time enough for sleep in the crowded discomfort of the mail coach. "But let me give you an extra pair of wool socks."

"Such favors." She looked up at him from under her eyelashes and Jack wished he had diamonds and gold to lay at her feet and not just wool stockings. "I will endeavor not to let it spoil me."

"Impossible," he assured her.

Everything about them was impossible. That they had finally found each other had seemed impossible mere days ago. That she would come to him and be his lover should have been impossible. But that she liked him just as much as he liked her was the most impossible thing of all.

It was nothing short of miraculous.

"Come, my love, let us away."

They took the way she had suggested slowly despite the cold, ambling along arm in arm as if it were a summer's day and not a bitter night in the depths of winter. As if they had all the time in the world instead of the last few moments they would ever spend together.

They took as long as possible, only reaching the toll-booth where the Queensferry Road gave way to Drumsheugh and then Kirk Brae Head as the first faint fingers of dawn began to light the eastern sky.

But it was there that their luck ran out—a crested town carriage rolled to a stop beside them. "Get in," Lady Ivers instructed acerbically. "Quickly, now. There's no time to lose."

Beside him, Flora's face turned ashen in the lamplight, but there was no sense in trying to cut and run, so he did as the lady instructed, assisting Flora into the snug carriage before he climbed up behind her and settled in for their keel hauling. "Good morning, my lady." He tipped his hat politely. "What exquisite timing you have. Dear Miss Conway's toes were growing cold."

Lady Ivers smiled but did not waver in her purpose. "Don't bother trying to charm me, Jack. It's five-thirty in the morning and I have not had the necessary pleasure of my chocolate."

"Our condolences, my lady," Flora put in kindly. "Why on earth are you out and about this time of morning?"

"Because a report of an alarming nature came to me, that you, Miss Flora Conway, were not come home at the appointed hour."

Color rose in his beloved's pale cheeks. "Raines ought to know better than to peach me out," Flora muttered.

"My dear girl, who did you think had trained the woman up and sent her your way when your father brought you north to Edinburgh?"

Flora looked non-plussed for only a moment. "Oh. That would have been you, my lady. Naturally."

"Indeed. And she remains as loyal to me as she is steadfast to you. So here we are." Lady Ivers looked at both of them evenly. "Although I know it to be impossible, because I expressly forbade it, I suppose I must wish you happy."

"We *are* very happy, my lady," Flora averred before Jack could affirm the same sentiment on his own. "But we will not marry," she continued calmly. "I have chosen not to lay that burden amongst the many others at my dear Captain Balfour's door."

Jack felt the soft stab of her statement like the sharpest pike. It was nothing but charity that she should phrase her words like that—as if he had made her an offer despite the exigencies of his circumstances.

That he had not done the gentlemanly thing and made that offer, stuck in his throat like bitterest gall.

But Flora was steadfast. "I am sorry we must disappoint you, my lady. But not every story ends with a fairy tale."

"No," the older woman agreed on a sigh. "Not everyone has the privilege of sailing off into the sunset, though I had hopes for you two."

A vain hope, in Jack's opinion. "No hidden asset or saving family treasure has, or will ever be found, my lady. We are a profligate bunch we Balfours, more successful as rogues and pirates than noblemen."

"Nonsense," Lady Ivers very kindly disagreed. "You are the finest of men. It is a blight on this county's history that your forebears should have made you poor."

"But poor I am, and poor I will continue to be. And poorer still I will be in a few days's time, if the Admiralty will take pity on me and allow me to fit out my ship on credit and the promise of my good name."

"A few days's time?" Lady Ivers asked. "Have we run out of rope? At Christmas?"

"Aye. Napoleon has not been idle during the season, ma'am," Jack informed her. "And in consequence neither has the Admiralty. Time is of the essence."

"I see. Yes, of course," she agreed. "I had not realized things had gotten to such a juncture so soon. I had hopes that this peace would hold." She reached out to pat Flora's hand in solace. "So, I will not try to keep you, but I will do what I can to keep Miss Conway for you."

"I thank you, my lady." He kissed her hand and then bowed very politely toward Flora. "Miss Conway."

"Jack, please. We have no secrets from Lady Ivers," Flora said before she turned away to check under the curtains. "But unfortunately, time has run out for me, as well—we have reached my house. My home," she said quietly. "And poor Raines is standing in the cold stable yard in wait. I must take leave of you both. My lady." She reached for Lady Ivers's hand. "You have my thanks. And Jack—"

She turned to him and it was everything he could do not to take her into his arms. Not to kiss her one last time.

But her composure seemed to be hanging from as thin a thread has his. "Dearest Jack. You have my heart and all my good wishes, along with my abiding friendship." She took up his hand a pressed a kiss to his gloved palm. "Godspeed."

And then she all but tumbled her way out the door without waiting for the carriage to come to a stop or the step to be put down.

And she was gone.

And he, for the first time in the entirety of his life, felt completely and utterly alone.

Almost. "Well, bollocks." Augusta Ivers heaved out a sigh. "That didn't end as I wanted." She shook her head as if to clear her thoughts. "Let me at least conduct you back to King's Circus Mews to collect your sea trunks."

"I thank you." Jack would take all the help he could get. "And perhaps I might trouble you to conduct me from there to the Grassmarket? The mail coach leaves on the dawn, but there are last minute preparations I must attend to. Notes and instructions for the lawyers. A new will to be signed so the estate, such as it is, has a clear path forward in the event of my death. You understand."

"I do," Lady Ivers swore solemnly. "My dear admiral did much the same whenever we went to sea. But I wonder…" She cast a speculative glance at him. "I'm for London myself in one day's time, but *my* preparations are all made. Why not do me the favor of traveling with me and spare yourself the inconveniences of the public mail coach. I assure you, my equipage will make the distance in better time than the mail. And far more comfortably."

Why not? What was one last luxury in the face of so much coming privation. Why should he not accept the one small gift fate was being generous enough to hand him. "That would be most agreeable, my lady. I accept."

"Excellent. I like it when you fall in with my plans for you, Jack. That's why I like you."

Jack bowed to her in tribute. "My lady, I live to serve."

"See that you do that, Jack. See that you do."

CHAPTER 16

*F*lora refused to repine. She would not stew in regret like the veriest pea-brained green girl. She would face the peril of his absence with calm confidence, secure in the knowledge that he had lived most of his life in the navy and had not yet come to harm. She would have faith. She would believe in him, if not wholly for her own sake, then for his.

And she would write to him. This minute.

She went to fetch paper, pen and ink, when the bell rang.

"Who can that be?" Raines asked as she left Flora's tea tray to answer the bell, and usher in a distinguished looking gentleman, his spectacles frosted with snow.

"Your pardon for the late call, miss." The gentleman swept his snowy hat from his white head. "Hector MacQueen, Esquire, of MacQueen, Reedy and Urquart."

The ancient fellow very correctly handed Raines his card for her to pass to Flora. "Solicitors to Captain Jonathan Balfour, Earl of Kinloch."

Panic flowed through her like acid. "What has happened?" Jack had only just left that morning! "Has there been some accident upon the road?"

"Do not distress yourself, Miss Conway."

"But why are you here?" Flora blurted before she recalled herself to her manners. "Pray forgive me, but this is most unexpected."

"I have come with this small posey that the Earl of Kinloch tasked me with ordering for you, Miss Conway, as a small token of his esteem."

"Captain Balfour's esteem?" Flora took the flowers reverently. "You are very kind."

"But I have not come solely to deliver you flowers, Miss Conway." The old gentleman looked about the corridor meaningfully. "If there is somewhere we might talk privately?"

Flora tried not to smile—how could the gentleman know she was in the house alone and kept only the barest of staff. "Yes, of course, do forgive me. Do come in. Raines, if you could bring Mr. MacQueen some refreshment in the library?" Raines would know well enough to bring the man whisky along with some tea.

Flora composed herself as she led the man into what had been her father's book room. She took a seat in one of the chairs in front of the desk and waved Mr. MacQueen into the other. "Now, Mr. MacQueen, how may I be of assistance to you?"

"It is I who have come in assistance to you, ma'am." He opened his folded leather portfolio and briefly consulted a paper therein. "It is a very private, sensitive matter, Miss Conway, but you may be assured of my discretion." He repositioned his spectacles upon the tip of his nose. "The Earl of Kinloch has changed his personal will—that portion of his personal estate that does not pertain to the Earldom and Estate of Kinloch, which are, as you might expect, quite thoroughly entailed."

"Of course." Flora was non-plussed. "And how can this concern me, sir?"

"It is a matter of some delicacy, Miss Conway, which is why I thought it best to visit you in the privacy of your home. You see, the earl, in his capacity as Captain Balfour, has made you a bequest of his personal estate and effects should he pass away at sea."

There was nothing that could have prepared her to receive such astonishing news. She could not have heard the man rightly over the sudden pounding of her blood in her ears.

"But I thought he was poor and had no ..." Flora searched for a word that did not make her seem like the veriest fortune hunter. "I was under the understanding that the Kinloch estate had consumed all of the captain's personal assets?"

"Nearly all," Mr. MacQueen said with some small satisfaction. "We were able to keep a small, but not entirely insignificant, asset—chiefly a piece of freehold property—apart from the Kinloch Earldom."

"Oh, I see," she said, though she did not really see at all.

"The earl, Captain Balfour, had meant for his behest to remain a secret until such time as his demise, but I thought it best—right and necessary—to inform you of his wishes." The man hesitated and lowered his voice. "There are one or two particulars that I should like to clarify for the documents to be correct. Normally, I would deal with your father for such a legal matter, but it is understood that Mr. Conway is without the country at this juncture?"

"Yes, my father is away. But I am of age, Mr. MacQueen."

"But under the law…" Mr. McQueen hesitated again. "Is there not some other gentleman that your father stipulated to act upon your behalf?"

"I am not permitted to act upon my own behalf?" Flora knew the legalities involved, but still, it rankled that she should have so little real autonomy. "Perhaps my brother-in-law, Lord Archibald Carrington, son of the Marquess of Aiken, would be the correct person?"

Mr. MacQueen's face cleared at this news. "Excellent. That will do nicely. The conveyance of the small personal property on Kings Circus Mews is not, in the grand scheme of things, a large bequest, but the resultant funds from the sale will provide a tidy little independent annual income."

"How…thoughtful." Flora felt her face heat, even as she strove to speak evenly. "May I ask… That is, if you are privy to Captain Balfour, that is the Earl of Kinloch's intentions… Why should he do such a thing?"

"Indeed." Mr. MacQueen cleared his throat. "While it is my duty to keep the earl's wishes confidential, the unusual circumstances—his service at sea—compelled me to visit. His exact words—I wrote them down quite exactly, you may be assured, Miss Conway."

"Yes?"

"He said that he should have liked to be able to marry by his own preference if circumstances had permitted, and he wanted some token of his esteem to be made in the absence of that ability."

"If circumstances had permitted?" she heard herself repeat.

"Yes, Miss Conway," the older gentleman affirmed. "Had the Earldom of Kinloch not been bankrupt, the earl might have been able to follow his own inclinations. But as it stands, he felt he could not, in all responsibility, burden a bride with such debts as his."

"I understand," was all she might manage.

"I thought you should know, Miss Conway." Mr. MacQueen stood. "And just to allay any concerns you might have, I can assure you that this matter will be kept with the utmost confidence. No one but you and his Lordship will know about the arrangement."

"Yes, thank you. I—" She meant to stand and offer the man her hand and act like a woman of sense and not some green girl. But she was rooted to her seat. "It is very good of you to tell me."

But the knowledge, the idea, that Jack had in the last moment he was here, thought of her and gone so far as to act upon his impulse was… remarkable to say the least. Thoughtful. Gentlemanly.

He would be such a man. Even at the last.

Flora felt her eyes sting with the tell-tale heat of tears. She brushed them away, but clearly, the impression she had made on him was not half as such as he had made upon her.

But what on God's ice-covered earth was she going to do about that?

JACK WALKED INTO THE WAITING ROOM ON THE admiralty's Levee Day with leaden feet, dragging himself through the door and into the crowded hall by dint of will and self-discipline alone.

The place was full of milling sailors, ranking from the lowest boys to post captains such as himself. He tipped his hat to one such fellow, an older man who had sat his lieutenancy exams with Jack a lifetime ago and done either so poorly—or so well—that he had been put into a bomb-ketch and never been given the chance to command anything better.

Such was life in the Navy—years of meritorious service in his lowly bomb-ketch and still, here the poor man was, hat in hand.

As was he.

Jack swiped off said hat and stowed in neatly under his arm while he signed in, writing only "Cpt Balfour" and the year he made post. The list, he was frightened to note, contained a good hundred names before him.

He found an empty foot of wall space, leaned upon his back, and settled down to wait.

"Captain, Lord Kinloch?" a stentorian voice called not thirty seconds later.

"Balfour," he corrected automatically, as he rose and went toward the clerk. "Captain Jack Balfour, although also, uselessly, Lord Kinloch."

"Yes, my lord captain." The clerk did not appreciate his humor. "This way."

Jack cast an apologetic glance at the myriad other fellows who had formerly been milling about the place like a school of barracudas. They had come to a standstill now, staring at him with undisguised hostility. "My apologies," Jack offered lamely. "No accounting for taste."

"Or influence," someone muttered.

Jack gave up on trying to plead poverty and left them to their imprecations, following the clerk down a set of labyrinthine corridors before he was shown into a small, sunny apartment where he was astonished to see his friend Sir Charles Middleton sat behind a desk, poring over a list.

"Balfour!" he called, waving Jack over. "Good to see you, my friend. How have you been faring?" He eyed Jack up and down with open concern. "You look as if you've been hauling sharp—you've lost a few stone, if I'm not mistaken. The rumors must be true about your bankrupt earldom."

"Your intelligence is, as usual, impeccable, sir."

Sir Charles let out a laugh, but swiftly moved on to the business at hand. "We've put you to a frigate. The Dutch are, no doubt, waiting for their moment to strike out from the Low Countries while the French will attempt to break out of Brest. Napoleon, I know I need not tell you, is but hours from breaking his peace. I need you out there—North Sea, North Atlantic, it makes no difference to me. I will rely upon your instincts for where you are best needed, though Nelson, who has nothing but praise for you, will likely want you against the Dutch. I can offer you a fifth rate, *Resistance*, 18 pounder, 36-guns, decent sailer. Or an Apollo class fifth rate, *Hotspur*, also 36 guns, sails like a hog."

Jack did not hesitate. "*Resistance*. And the crew? Are there officers attached to her, or may I appoint my own?"

"A smattering of each, to my knowledge—a skeleton crew at the very least and two capable young lieutenants. Sailing Master on *Resistance* is a forty-year man, John Gallery. Excellent man. Never steer you wrong."

"*Resistance*, it is." The name seemed fitting.

"Balfour?" Sir Charles peered over his glasses at Jack. "Is that…resignation I hear? Thought you'd be over the moon to get a ship so quickly with so many men waiting."

"Oh, I am sensible of the honor, sir."

"But?" Sir Charles asked bluntly.

"But I wish it were not necessary. I'm afraid I've grown accustomed to safety and calm, and I no longer relish putting my head out as a target for a cannonball."

The older man chuckled. "You won't say that when you're out there, besting the enemy again."

"Perhaps not. Definitely not, if I know what's good for my men and my ship. But the truth is, my heart's gone out of it."

Sir Charles Middleton let out an oath so blue, Jack was astonished that the room didn't fill with cold mist. "I'm sorry," he finally said. "But there's nothing for it. We need you. The Admiralty needs its best men, and that, my boy, is you."

Jack took a deep breath and stood. "I know my duty, sir."

"Good. As do I, for if I sent you back out into the world in defiance of Lady Augusta Ivers's express orders, I wouldn't like my chances."

"Lady Ivers interfered, did she?"

"Lady Ivers strongly recommended. And I respect both her late husband, and her own acuity, too much to doubt her opinion is sound." But Sir Charles had his own acuity—he leveled his eyes on Jack. "But you may rest your worries that you have not been given favor solely on your own merit and abilities. Lady Ivers's recommendation only piled on more canvas—we had already written you, when her letter told us to expect you."

"And here I am."

"And here, you are, at last. Doing what you were meant to do."

"Taught to do, certainly," Jack joked. "Who knows— perhaps, left to my own devices, I would have made a hell of a farmer."

"Come, man," Sir Charles cajoled. "You're a hell of a captain, and you know it."

"Just because I'm good at it doesn't mean I have to like it."

"Agreed," Sir Charles returned. "They say a man who will go to sea for pleasure will go to hell for pastime. But like it or not, that's up to you. There's glory in it for you, either way."

"I'll defer any glory if I may. You can give it all to Vice-Admiral Nelson." Jack named the former shipmate who seemed most destined for glory. "He's made for it, the poor man."

"So are you if you want it."

Jack respected Middleton too much not to give him the truth. "And I most assuredly do not."

Sir Charles's laugh was rueful. "Then the only problem, my boy, is however shall you avoid it."

CHAPTER 17

"*F*lora? Are you here?"

"Maisie?" Flora was roused out of her unhappy reverie—she had not even heard the bell ring, or the door latch open.

"Yes," her sister answered as she made her uneven way through the library doorway. "And Archie, too."

"Flora," was all her brother-in-law said in greeting. Which was strange for such a 'hail-fellow-well-met' sort of man. Who, now that she took the time to notice, was giving Flora a strange, narrow-eyed stare.

"What goes on?" she asked. "It's Raines's half-day off, so I can't even offer you—" Flora broke off when Maisie sat next to her on the divan and reached for her hand. "What is wrong?"

"I'm afraid it's bad news, dearest."

Flora felt herself go cold with dread and hot with

fear in sickening succession. "What happened? No, don't tell me!" The fear that had lived inside her like a live fox since her visit from Jack's lawyer began to gnaw at her insides. "Is he dead?"

"Yes," Maisie said simply and quietly. "I'm so sorry."

But before her sister had even finished her sentence, Flora had begun to weep—crying with great wracking sounds that felt purged from the depth of her being. Aching pain gripped her lungs and throat, and she could not draw breath.

"No," she cried. And again, "No. I should have never let him go."

"Let him go?" Maisie looked confused. "I thought we all agreed his departure was for the best—"

"No." Flora choked out between sobs. "It wasn't for the best. He only went because of the debt."

"What debt?" Archie asked, looking from Maisie to Flora and back again. "There is no indication of any outstanding debt." He came close to Flora, as if to assure her. "Your home and livelihood are quite secure. You needn't fear."

It wasn't fear that had her in its grips, but sorrow. Sorrow and hideous gnawing grief that opened up a hole where her heart used to be. The pain—the physical pain of not existing in the same world as him—was nearly intolerable.

"Forgive me, dearest." Maisie wrapped her arms

around Flora's shoulders. "We should have broken it to you more gently."

"No, please." Flora was not ashamed of her own tears, but she would not let Maisie shoulder any blame. "There was nothing else you could do but give me the awful truth."

"Perhaps." Maisie was still frowning, but she held Flora's hand tenderly. "I thought, or hoped, that distance would lessen the pain. That his prolonged absence would make it easier to bear in the end."

"No," Flora insisted. "Not easier to bear. Worse. Much worse. I never should have let him go."

Maisie's confusion began to give way to some small perturbation. "Please forgive my asking, but did you not suggest he return to plant finding for the company, yourself? I swear we stood right here in this very room—"

Flora gulped to a stop. It was her turn to be utterly confused. "What are you talking about?"

Maisie stared at her. "Papa leaving Edinburgh in the wake of the debacle that was his time as the Lord Advocate."

Flora felt has if her head were about to split in two. "What does that have to do with Jack?"

"Jack Balfour?" Archie queried. "Post Captain Balfour of the Royal Navy, Jack? Jack, the Earl of Kinloch?"

"Yes?" Flora looked from one to the other. "Who are you talking about?"

"Papa," Maisie said, enunciating clearly, as if Flora had somehow misheard her.

Flora felt the tight band that had closed about her chest give way enough to breathe. A little. For a moment. "Do you mean to tell me Papa is dead?"

"Yes." Maisie rubbed Flora's hand this time, as if she could press the truth into it.

"Oh, no." Her feelings were such a tumult that she began to laugh and cry all at the same time. "I thought you meant— Oh, thank God." She hiccupped and swiped at her wet cheeks with the edge of her sleeve. "I mean, I am sorry. Oh, poor Papa. But I just thought it was far worse." She took the handkerchief Archie so solicitously handed to her. "Forgive me, please. I'm all at sixes and sevens. I hardly know myself."

"Yes," Maisie agreed. "We hardly know you either." She glanced back at Archie for a moment. "But there is more."

"More? How much more? Good or bad more?"

"It depends on one's perspective, I suppose," Maisie said philosophically. "But the long and short of it is, that Papa, for all his faults and foibles—"

"More faults than foibles, I would judge," Flora countered. "Bless the poor man."

"Agreed." Maisie nodded. "But for his sins, he seems to have left us, you and I, quite a tidy fortune."

Flora was flummoxed—what on earth did that mean? "A tidy fortune?" she repeated.

"Yes," Maisie confirmed. "I had no idea his finances were so…" She spread her hands. "That his fortune was…" She hesitated, as if she was looking for the right adjective.

"Enormous," Archie supplied. "Shares of the East India Company. A vast number. Enough to make him, and now you two, *nabobs*."

The word conjured up far away, opulent, colorful treasures. "We—" Flora gestured back and forth Maisie and herself. "—are rich?"

"Yes," Maisie said.

"How rich?"

"Again," Archie said with a roguish tilt of his head, "enormously so. Never-have-to-work-a-day-in-your-life-again sort of rich. Could-eat-your-money-for-breakfast-and-supper-and-still-not-run-out-of-it rich."

Flora was beyond amazement. "He never said a thing." She gaped at her sister. "Did he say anything to you?"

"No." Maisie said. "It makes me wonder about all the other things he never said." She sighed. "But I suppose we'll never know, now."

"No going back, now. No regrets," Archie advised his wife. "Only going forward."

"Yes, we must go forward," Maisie said with some firmness.

There was something equally stunned and determined on Maisie's face that could not come from her grief about Papa—she had suffered too much neglect under his care to really mourn his passing.

"What is it?" Flora pulled herself out of her own swirl of emotions to have a care for Maisie's. "You needn't feel guilty, dearest heart, you know, if you're not particularly unhappy—"

"No." Maisie shook her head. "Certainly not. But…"

"But what?"

"After *everything*"—Maisie alluded to Flora's former pledge not to marry until she had seen her sister happy—"I am just so very glad for your sake that you are finally free to do as *you* please." Maisie spread her hands in front of her as if to say all things were now possible. "From now on, you need not please anyone but yourself."

"And society." Money was certainly a great leveler of obstacles. But there were expectations of women that held sway no matter if one were rich or poor.

"No!" Maisie was adamant. She reached again for Flora's hand, as if she would press her urgency upon her sister. "No, certainly not. Not if you don't want to. I know that the lawyers will eventually tell you that Archie and I—but mostly Archie—are to be your trustees, but you are of age, and neither Archie nor I intend to give you anything more than advice when asked, and our blessing, no matter if we are asked or not."

"What are you not saying?"

"That finally, *you* may do as *you* like."

"As I like?" Flora hardly knew where to begin. "Could we sell this house? Might I take a house for myself somewhere more to my taste and inclination?"

"Yes. There is more than enough money. He was a canny investor, your wily old Papa," Archie commented.

"Yes, although *I* might want to buy this house just for the attic studio," Maisie sent a warm smile toward her husband. "I rather miss the quality of the light there."

"I might take a place in the New Town, I suppose," Flora conceded. Somewhere near King's Circus. Somewhere exactly like King's Circus—the property directly in front of the mews at number twenty-six.

"You may buy yourself half of the Highlands, and still have money left over. Or you could go back to Richmond—I know you loved it there. Just as you choose," Maisie confirmed. "I mean it, Flora—you may, truly and finally, do what you like for yourself. You may make yourself happy."

Hardly. Money might buy her a house, or a Highland

estate, but it could not buy happiness. She could not bring the only man she feared she was ever going to love, let alone *like* enough to marry, back to her.

"For example, we should like to set up a charity, Archie and I," Maisie was saying. "And we would very much like you to be a partner in that venture, if you like."

"Yes," Flora agreed, for one's good fortune ought to be shared. "Of course. We'll do what is right and useful. Do all the good we can." This perhaps, could be her purpose.

"Yes!" Maisie warmed to her favorite topic. "I'm so glad you agree. We'll join forces with Quince, Lady Cairn—endow her charity with a working fund, don't you think? Best not to reinvent the wheel. But I should like to also help cottagers with debts, so they might keep their land and cottages, instead of trying to help them after they've lost everything. As well as those—"

Flora was already standing bolt upright by the time her brain caught up with her body. "Debts?"

"Yes." Maisie was back to her fierce frowning. "So many people get trapped in a cycle of poverty by excessive debt, often that they inherit—"

"My God." Flora was the one who grappled for Maisie's hand this time. Within her chest, her heart began to beat a staccato rhythm as the idea began to take hold of her. "I could pay off the debt."

"Yes," Archie agreed cautiously. "But as I told you, there is no debt on the house, or attached to your name. Your father was negligent in some areas, but he seems to have been quite meticulous with his finances. There are no debts."

"I was rather thinking of someone else's debts. A…" Did she dare say it out loud? Did she dare give name to her dream? "A friend—or a husband's debt," she amended.

Maisie stared at her. "I thought you had gone off the idea of a husband?"

"I did. I mean, I …" Flora looked back to Archie. "But an enormous sum? One that might buy a Highland estate like…"

"Kinloch?" Archie looked at Maisie, and then back at Flora. "Like Jack Balfour's debts?" He asked quietly.

"Yes." Flora was too relieved to be embarrassed. "Exactly like. How did you know?"

"A discreet visit from a certain solicitor, a Mr. McQueen," Archie stated.

"And we have eyes, my dearest," Maisie's tone was more than kind—it was patient and loving. "You with your spun-gold fineness and he with his brooding dark? Our world is a curious place where opposites inevitably attract."

"But he is not my opposite," Flora asserted. Nothing

could be farther from the truth. They were so alike. "He is my soulmate."

"Ah, then." Maisie smiled even as her eyes went suspiciously misty. "Then we had best do all that we can to get you two together. But then his debts really are as bad as rumored?"

"Worse, I'm sure," Flora said, "for I have only Jack's offhand comments about the 'bankrupt earldom.' But I refuse to think of them as Jack's debts—as he so pithily once said, he didn't even have the pleasure of accruing them."

"Just so," Maisie said quietly. "Flora, dearest, why don't we all go down to the kitchen to get a nice cup of tea, which we will absolutely lash with whisky—or brandy, just as you choose—and you can tell us all about your friend, Captain Jack Balfour."

"Yes." Flora felt her mood begin to brighten. "Why don't we do just that. And you two extraordinarily devious plotters can help me come up with a plan to win him back."

CHAPTER 18

*T*heir plan, such as it was, began with the frustratingly mundane—banking accounts.

Maisie insisted that before any other action might be taken, she and Flora spend several long, but ultimately fascinating days with Papa's banker and man of business, Mr. Henry Dundas, who gave them a thorough education in the management and maintenance of their new private fortunes.

And although the wizened Mr. Dundas first protested the lack of a male chaperone and advisor during their session, he soon warmed to Maisie's very sound idea to make them more financially literate—especially Flora, whom he saw as vulnerably unmarried.

"Per the law, Lord Archibald Carrington will serve as primary trustee of your funds, Miss Conway, but I should advise you to understand and participate in every particular." Mr. Dundas proceeded to patiently show them each balance book of asset and expenditure, until Flora at last felt she had a grasp upon the importance of the responsibility—as well as the possibilities—before her.

"I should also advise you," Dundas went on, "as I would my own daughters, to bring some trusted women—in particular, widows who have proved expert at the managing of their own estates—into your confidence as advisors as well. To guide you in the ways of being a woman of fortune."

"Lady Ivers perhaps?" Flora suggested.

"Excellent woman," was Mr. Dundas's opinion. "Precisely whom I might have suggested."

"And perhaps the Marchioness of Cairn?" Maisie added.

"She is not a widow," Dundas considered. "And yet, she is well-known for her management of her charities, which, her esteemed husband—who is well known to us at the Bank of Scotland— tells me, she directs all on her own. A very good choice, indeed," was his final assessment.

"I think we understand your intent, sir," Maisie said when they finally put away all the balance books. "And we thank you for both your time and your advice."

"You are most welcome. My only other counsel," he said in conclusion, "would be to avoid rushing into anything at the present juncture. To wait for the fresh surprise and astonishment of coming into a fortune to wear off a bit before you purchase anything."

"Thank you, Mr. Dundas." Flora extended her hand for him to shake. "But I have already made up my mind. In fact, my mind was set some time ago. I mean to spend my money purchasing the estate of the Earl of Kinloch. And I won't be swayed. But I shall keep all your advice and attention to the balance sheet in mind when I do so and drive a very hard bargain." She gave the poor man the full measure of the swivel gun of her smile. "I understand the Bank of Scotland owns the notes. What can you offer me?"

Dundas was of such a character that he did not quaver. "My dear Miss Conway." He rubbed his hands together in relish. "Let us call in the books."

"Raines!" Flora called as soon as she made it back to the house. "I'm going to London!"

In order to fight for him, she had to find him first.

"Raines!" She began pulling her best traveling clothes from the armoire—what did one wear when one went in pursuit of the love of one's life? Ought she to look the heiress? "Raines!"

"I heard you the first time, miss," Cora Raines said with some asperity as she bustled into the room and immediately began picking up the clothes that Flora was pulling out. "And *we* are going to London, Miss Flora," Raines countered. "I promised Lady Ivers I'd look after you and look after you I bloody well shall. Give me that." The maid scooped a tweed redingote out of her hands. "You'll crease it something horrible, wadding it up like that."

"Time is of the essence," Flora countered. "There's no time for careful packing. We need—"

"By the time you go downstairs to speak to cook about a hamper and go to the stables to speak to young Davie, I'll have us packed and ready to get you changed into suitable traveling attire. I'll not have you haring off, looking like some north country bumpkin who doesn't know how to dress, I'll tell you…"

Flora did not wait to hear the rest of Raines' diatribe on offenses against fashion but followed her direction and made for the kitchens and stables. And when she returned, there were as promised, three small trunks in the corridor and a fresh traveling suit of winter tartan spread out on the bed.

"You'll want short stays for travel," Raines advised. "Won't be as elegant, but far more comfortable. And truth is you're elegant enough to knock the boots off any man, even when you're not at your best."

"I'm never seen at less than my best," Flora swore. "I refuse to be."

"That's my lass," Raines answered.

They were away within a half an hour, but the furious flurry of activity that hastened their departure soon lapsed into the tedium of the days-long journey. The post inns with their lumpy beds and hastily eaten hot stews blended from one into the other until at last, they braked to an exhausted stop in front of Lady Ivers's London townhouse on Manchester Square.

But Flora's foot had not even hit the pavement alighting from the coach when Lady Ivers herself came streaming out of the house.

"Thank God you're here. You've not a moment to spare. He'll be off from Portsmouth within the next day or two, I've no doubt. I did my best to delay him, insisting upon the delivery of one thing or another which he dared not wait for, but I ran out of excuses."

"Excuses for what?"

"Excuses for him not to go to sea! Excuses for him to come back home to Edinburgh where he belongs, with you!" Lady Ivers said with considerable frustration, as if Flora didn't want exactly the same thing.

"Well, all right then," she agreed. "I will go to him, this instant. But I will need fresh horses, if you can spare them?" She confirmed this with a glance at the driver. "Yes? And if you would but tell me where I am to go to find him—?"

"Portsmouth. The ship *Resistance*. Ask along the Navy dockyard and they should be able to direct you. Aim the carriage for the masts and spars of the harbor and you can't go wrong."

"All right." Flora nodded more confidently that she felt. "I will be away as soon as the horses may be changed."

"Yes, good," Lady Ivers agreed. "We'll see to that." She gestured hurriedly to her major domo who immediately hustled off to parts interior.

"And if I may leave my maid, Raines, with you here, for she is done in by the travel and needs must rest. I shall go on—"

"Not alone!" Lady Ivers was vehement. "Of course, you shall need to be alone with him at the salient moment. Of course. But between now and then—!" She cast about for only a moment before she made her decision. "I shall come with you—no!" She instantly changed her mind. "You shall come with *me* in my coach—well sprung, fresh horses, and a fresh but experienced man at the reins. Your boy must be even more exhausted than your maid. Come in while I make arrangements. Don't argue—"

"I will not." Flora said as she made for the door. "I

accede to your plan quite easily. I put myself in your capable hands."

"Excellent." Lady Ivers finally drew a breath. "I knew you would come in time to save him. I felt it in my bones. I just knew."

CHAPTER 19

*P*ortsmouth, which looked so serene and still from afar, was a raucous, clamoring forest of moving masts up close, all swaying dizzily this way and that.

"*Resistance*, ma'am," called down the coachman as he pulled up alongside what appeared to be an empty quay.

Flora alighted in confusion at the vast array of ships anchored before her. "Where?" She asked stupidly, before clarifying, "Which ship?"

The coachman set his brake before clamoring down so he wouldn't have to shout over the wind. "That one, I should think, ma'am," he said pointing to the veritable sea of ships riding at anchor. "The porter at the dockyard gate said frigate, which are two deckers." He pointed more specifically to the cluster of double-decked ships. "Middle of those three, he said. Chancer!" He called to the boy still up on the box. "Escort Miss Conway down to the sally port there and find her a boatman to call out to *Resistance*. Reckon you can send a message that way, miss."

"Thank you." But she would not merely send a message. Not when it would be so much more expedient to send herself. She much preferred to deliver her own messages—especially since she had not yet thought of exactly what she was to say.

At the sally port, which was only a series of stone steps down to the water, an old woman with a face as wrinkled and raw as an apple core sat at the oars of a small boat tethered by a rope to an iron ring on the quay.

"*Resistance*, you want?" The crone looked vaguely in the direction of the ships riding at anchor. "Tell you which one for a shilling. Take you out to her for only six bob more."

"Yes, please, immediately," Flora answered, fishing the necessary coins out of her purse.

"Miss?" The boy shifted nervously. "What will I tell Lady Ivers?"

"Tell her I shall return with my prize posthaste," Flora said stoutly, before adding, "And you may tell her prayers are appreciated, but not necessary."

"Listen to you. Sitcher'self down, Duchess," the old woman cackled. "Wand we'll be well away."

If Flora had felt tossed and turned in the carriage, the present sensation of being on the sea was somehow softer but all the more violent. And if the wind in Edinburgh had been raw, the cutting gale off the sea was practically arctic.

"What'cher want wiff *Resistance?*" the water-woman queried as she rowed unerringly toward the central of the three ships at anchor without ever once turning to check over her shoulder for her direction.

"I have some business there," Flora said as cryptically as possible, huddling into her cloak. One really didn't want to broadcast one's proposal like the commonest fishwife. But if the water-woman felt free with her curiosity, then so might Flora. "How does a woman come to take this job?"

"No men left for it, are there? All gone to His Majesty's service round these parts, what wiff room, board and grub included in the navy. I'd go there meself, if they'd take me," she cackled. "But I earn a decent enuff living here." She gestured to her oars. "And I like me work. Set me own hours. Better'n cleaning up slops fer some 'igh and mighty mistress. Beggin' your pardon, Duchess."

Flora merely nodded because her attention was all taken up by the ship looming nearer.

"Ahoy, *Resistance!*" The old lady tar cawed as the boat

drew alongside the high wall of the frigate. "What's yer name, Duchess?"

"Flora Conway. Miss."

"*Miss* Flora Conway for—" The water-woman paused and raised her hoary eyebrows at Flora, waiting for her to supply her business with the ship.

"For Captain Balfour," Flora managed, though her tongue suddenly felt thick and dry.

"*Miss* Flora Conway 'as business with Cap'n Balfour," the harridan bellowed loud enough for all of the ship and half of the harbor to hear.

So much for discretion.

A half-dozen bare heads popped over the bulwarks above, staring down at her before one bearing a cocked bicorn came to the break in the rail and stared down before hurrying away. Another dozen or so sailors began to appear like birds alighting in the trees, slinging themselves out on the chain wale and the ratlines above.

"Who?" Came a deeply incredulous voice. "No, do not repeat that."

Sharp footsteps hurried down what sounded like a set of stairs before he appeared above her.

And there he was. "Jack!"

"Miss Conway." He touched his hat absent-mindedly as he stared at her for a moment before he recalled himself to his ship. "Damn your eyes," he growled at the nearest men. "Get off that rail and get back to work.

Find something to do before I find it for you. Mr. Stevens, see to the people." And then he stepped closer, standing full in the gap of the railing above, so she could see him in all his naval glory.

"You're looking well," she said apropos of nothing but wanting—needing—to say something.

He was not complimented. Or amused. "What are you doing here?"

Flora took a deep breath and did what he had once so cavalierly instructed her—she aimed the swivel gun of her smile at him and took her shot. "I've come to save you, if I may."

"Save me?" His frown furrowed deeper, but he unbent a little, leaning toward her a bit. "From what?"

"From the future," she tried, as her breath sent up frosted semaphore into the chill air between them. "Or the Navy. Or the French. Or Dutch. However you prefer."

A small hint of amusement began to brew at the corner of his mouth. "I don't need saving, Miss Conway."

"Flora," she reminded him. "And don't be absurd, Jack, of course you do, for you'd never leave on your own accord to save yourself."

"And I am meant to leave upon yours?" His brows rose so high she was surprised they didn't knock his hat off his head. "My dear Miss Conway, you clearly don't know how the Admiralty or the Royal Navy works."

"I am very glad to hear that I am your dear Miss Conway. And you are right, of course, I don't know anything about the Royal Navy. But I do know how the world works—and that is, I have an alternative to the Navy to propose to you."

She had his full and undivided attention now—he put his hands on either side of the bulwark and leaned down, as if he thought he had not heard her correctly. "An alternative?"

"Yes," she promised.

A long moment of silence followed—the only sounds were the lap and fall of the water against the boat and the side of the hull and the raucous shrill cry of the passing gulls—before he cleared his throat. "And what is that alternative?"

"Me." Flora decided not to say anything more. Not until he came down to her.

So, she waited.

Another silence, filled with the sounds of the harbor, the groaning ropes of the ship, and the bated breath of a few hundred men idling somewhere just out of eyeshot, ensued.

"Jack?"

"Forgive me, Miss Conway," he responded with

alacrity. "But I have not the pleasure of understanding you. Would you mind—"

"Would you mind coming down here to talk to me—for I'll never make it up there with anything like grace." She eyed the side of the hull rising and falling at an alarming rate not four feet from where she sat on her uncomfortable thwart. "The water looks frightfully cold. And I'm getting an awful crick in my neck trying to propose to you."

He immediately turned his back and for a sickening second Flora thought he meant to leave her. But instead, he began to quickly descend the side via the extraordinarily shallow foothold cobbled onto the side of the hull.

"Careful," she called.

"Miss Conway," he said as he reached the launch and turned to her. "I am always careful when I am being proposed to."

"Very sensible," she agreed while trying in vain not to smile like the veriest loon. "As you should be."

"As I am." He cast a glance at the water-woman. "Do you mind? If you'll wait aboard?" He passed her what Flora could only hope was adequate coin, for the old woman grumped her surprisingly spry way up the imaginary ladder and disappeared.

Jack sat himself in her place and bent himself to the oars. "For some small bit of privacy," he explained as he

175

rowed them away from the ship. But after such a promising start, he seemed to be heading them back the way she and the water-woman had just come.

"Where are you going? What about her?"

"I am taking you back to the quay and the land, where you belong," he explained tersely. "I'll bring the boat back for her, after."

After she had done what she came here to do. "I do belong there, with you," she insisted. "As I was hoping you belonged, too. With me," she clarified, since he was being obstreperous. "Please stop," she asked. "And please don't make me beg. Even though you know I will."

He finally did so, shipping the oars, letting the craft bob up and down idly upon the frigid waves. "So," he crossed his arms over his chest in that uncomfortable, impervious way of his. "What exactly are you begging, or proposing, Miss Conway?"

"It's Flora," she attempted one last time. "And I beg that you do me the honor and privilege of taking my hand in marriage."

CHAPTER 20

*J*ack stared at her, his straightforward, divine, keen lover, with as unflinching a stare as he could manage, even as his heart throttled within his chest. "Generally, a man likes to do his own proposing, Flora."

She rewarded him with a beaming smile. "Does he? So does a woman," she agreed pleasantly. "And although I will acknowledge that men generally have had the honor of asking, I should like to make it clear that women have generally already made their decision before things get to that point, so who does the asking is merely a matter of tradition—"

"And pride," he added. Such a damnable amount of pride.

"Yes." She nodded solemnly. "And I thank you for

recognizing mine. Because I am a prize worthy of a great deal of pride. Now, more than ever."

He had smiled at her quip—he had always liked how she knew her own worth—until the moment when his brain heard the last part of her declaration. "Now? And why is that?"

"I will gladly tell you why—for I think you will like it —but first, I should like an answer to my proposal."

The heat that had kindled within him at her first declaration flared anew. But he could not allow himself to hope. It would break his already wounded heart.

So, he shrugged and pulled a face that he hoped was full of amused cynicism. "You haven't really made your proposal—if you're going to do it traditionally."

"Of course." She came to her knees in the icy water swilling in the bottom of the boat and reached out to him. "My dearest, Jack," she said as she clasped his hands in hers. "Will you please make me the happiest of women and do me the undeserved honor of becoming my husband, to have and hold, from this day forward, in sickness and in health, for richer…"

"…or *poorer*," he finished for her. No matter what he wanted—and he wanted her more than air or water or life itself—he could not let her forget that choosing him would only be to her detriment. "Very much poorer, Flora. Which is why—"

"I'm afraid not," she disagreed quickly, cutting his

refusal off. "For I'm quite rich now. My father has died, you see, leaving my sister and I quite full up with shares of the East India Company. Which we have already sold, for ethical reasons, in case that matters to you. But which in any case, has left us quite, quite rich. Rich enough to marry where I want, not where I must."

"Are you quite serious?" He scowled at her, searching her face for the ravages of grief and pain. But though she did look somehow older, she did not however, look ravaged. "My condolences."

"Thank you." She squeezed his hand. "But I want your agreement far more than I want your condolences."

"But—" For the first time in the whole of their acquaintance—although calling one's lover to whom one was proposing an acquaintance didn't seem quite right—Jack felt entirely at a loss. "When?"

"When did he pass? Some months ago, we assume, for it took a long time for the news to reach us. But I came as soon as I found out. I wasn't going to tell you," she confessed. "I wanted you to make your decision based on me, alone. On your feelings for me, that is, alone. But it didn't seem fair, that you shouldn't know. So you could choose for yourself. So we could both choose what we want, instead of simply being chosen."

That she was as insightful as she was beautiful and honest ought not to startle him so now. But still, she stole his breath and his heart away.

"I don't mind being chosen by you," he told her. "In fact, I prefer it."

Her cheeks blossomed with hope. "Is that a yes?"

"Aye," he confirmed. His heart felt as if it would burst from him. Never had he had such hope. "I will marry you."

"Oh, Jack—" She threw her arms around his neck, raining kisses down upon his face.

He held her off, gently. "But, Flora, not now." He forced his head to reassert its dominance over his heart. "Not today. And certainly not for some small while."

"What do you mean?" She stilled, gripping his coat tight, as if loath to believe him, or let him go. "Why? Why not? Don't you love me?"

"I do love you. More than you will ever know." He reached out to touch her beautiful, sweet face because he wanted more than anything to hold her and show her how much he loved her. "But as much as I love you, I also have a duty that I cannot forsake. A ship that I cannot simply abandon."

"A duty you don't want," she was quick to point out.

"No—" he qualified. "That's not how duty works, Flora. I gave my word. The same as I give it to you. But I will renege on neither you nor the Admiralty."

"Can't you just resign?"

"No." He was adamant. "I have already received my orders for the Jutland Sea, which are made for me and me alone. I must return to my ship and my men and my duty and carry out my orders until such time as those orders are complete."

"But if you love me, why can't you simply tell them that you're done?"

"Because there is a duty that needs must be fulfilled now. The peace is about to break—Napoleon has been secretly violating his own treaties for some time now and is about to begin doing so openly. War must come. And I must be here to either prevent it or fight it. I have my orders."

Flora's eyes glistened with tears of frustration. "So, what is to be done?"

"I will return you to the quay and Lady Ivers's waiting carriage—for I can see her crest upon it, and I am very glad you have her with you. And I will return to my ship and my duty."

"But what about—? You needn't—" Tears began to spill down her rapidly paling cheeks. "I have money. We won't be poor."

His will began to waver in the sight of her pain. "I shall write to the Admiralty before I sail and see what can be done about our predicament," he conceded. "And we shall see what we shall see."

"But we won't see each other? We won't be together?" Her voice grew as raw as her cheeks.

"No," he agreed quietly. "Please, my dearest, do get up

off your knees in this bilge. Sit back in the stern sheets until I can row you ashore and kiss you goodbye properly."

"No," she refused. She instead leaned forward, reaching for his lapels and pulling his mouth down to hers with urgency and force. As if she could convince him that life with a willing young wife was infinitely preferable to barking orders at British tars.

And she had convinced him. But there was damn near nothing he could do about it at the moment.

So, he kissed her back. He kissed her with every ounce of hurt and hope he had stored away, hidden in the depths of his soul since he had left her. He kissed her with all of the want and attraction and desperate longing within him. With all the lust she had awakened within his body and all the love he felt in his breaking heart.

And she kissed him back with something close to abandon.

He took her up in his arms and in another moment, she was seated upon his lap with her legs crooked securely around his waist and her arms wrapped tightly around his back.

"Marry me, please," she begged.

"Certainly. Absolutely, I will," he answered between ragged breaths. "Soon. As soon as possible."

"Promise me you will," she demanded rather desperately.

Everything within him was being torn asunder by the hideous division between what he wanted and what he had to do. "I promise."

"Promise me you won't get killed," Flora begged.

"I promise," he pledged, although he couldn't promise anything of the kind. To stop her inevitable protest, he laid a cautionary finger across her lips to keep her from disagreeing. "I will promise you to be exceptionally careful. Although, you should know that more lives are lost to dirt and disease than ever are to cannonballs."

"You are not helping me to feel better," she cried. "Not in the least."

"Then I will promise that I will come home to you as soon as I bloody-well can. Because I do love you, and I do want to marry you." He took her face in his hands and held her away from him for a long moment, imprinting her upon his brain. Beautiful and wracked by the grief of worry, she was a mirror reflection of his own emotions. "I do love you," he repeated. "And I will marry you. Just not today."

He kissed her once more and set her away, turning her to sit beside him on the thwart while he tossed a rope to a boy standing by on the quay. "Take my betrothed's hand and help her ashore, man," he ordered as he did the same, taking her elbow to steady her way as she stepped from the boat onto the land.

"You're not coming ashore?" she protested. "Not even to see Augusta?"

"I am not." He shook his head. He dared not. "You may give her my regards, but only after you give me yours."

He pulled her roughly to him for one last searing kiss and just as roughly set her away on the uneven stone. "I'll write," he said rather tersely, as he sat back to the oars. "I love you. Goodbye."

CHAPTER 21

Flora had no choice but to take the hand of the groom who thankfully appeared by her side to lead her back to the carriage. Which she couldn't see because her eyes were filled with stinging tears.

"Tears?" Augusta Ivers reached out to help Flora out of the infernal, raw wind and into the cocooning shelter of the upholstered coach. "He's not coming?" She craned her head out the window to search the quay. "Whatever happened?"

"He's not coming," Flora confirmed. "Though he does love me. And he will marry me. When he comes back. If he comes back."

The dam of emotion Flora had kept in check through her sheer unbridled hope began to give way. Heat built in her eyes and pain gripped her throat. "Because I just know, now that I've found him and there is nothing standing in our way, he's surely going to go get himself killed."

Lady Ivers was having none of it. "You mustn't think like that. It won't do!" she counseled even as she gathered Flora to her side. "You must be the braver version of yourself, my dear girl—for your own sake as well as his. You must believe in him. You must."

"Yes, I will. I do." Flora gathered her aplomb and steadied her nerve. "I will conquer myself—for my own sake as well as his. You may depend upon that."

"That's my girl." Lady Ivers hugged her to her side.

"Yes," Flora said again, more to convince herself that her ladyship. "He will prevail. *We* will prevail. We will be together." She dried her tears and set her face toward the road. "Let us get on with it."

Despite her conviction, the journey back to Edinburgh was miserable, made more miserable by the inclement winter weather that doused them in freezing rain and set the countryside in frozen glass. But at least it matched her mood—from euphoria to brittle despair in one short, frenetic week.

Hope seemed impossible.

Flora reluctantly returned to the house on Kirk Brae Head to fret and wait and be miserable at home, where she at least had the comfort—and frustration—of the familiar. Every day she scanned the newspapers for some fresh news. And every day that she found it, she wished she had not.

Bonaparte was up to his old tricks, finding ways around enforcement of the Treaty of Amiens—and several other continental treaties, to boot—prompting the reactivation of the British blockade of the French coast. In response, Bonaparte made plain his renewed preparations for an invasion of Britain. The British Navy, it was being reported, were strengthening their Channel fleet, as well as massing ships at Great Yarmouth on the North Sea and at Malta, preparing to confront the Danes or the Dutch or the Italians, or repel the Russians, or prevent either from joining the much-feared emperor.

In other words, Jack was going directly into harm's way.

Every day it took hours for Flora to calm each fresh anxiety so she might feel and act herself. Thankfully, Maisie was a frequent visitor, as were Lady Ivers and Lady Cairn. They cheered and chuffed and encouraged her plans for a new house and her kept company and generally tried their best not to leave Flora too much time to brood and worry.

"Flora, dear, won't you come over to my studio—I've a fresh canvas in the works for the Countess of Argyle that I should like your opinion on. You have a wonderful eye for color and style. I've put her in a very lovely pale green, but with all the trees in the landscape behind, I am now wondering if she might be shown to better advantage in blue."

"Yes, certainly, I will come as soon as may be," Flora answered. Anything to keep her from sitting at home, occupied only by her thoughts. "And I'll bring Raines—it's her eyes that have trained mine."

And speaking of Raines, the bell at the door announced another visitor.

"That will be Archie, come to see me home," Maisie said. "How about dinner tomorrow evening, just the three of us—you, me, and Archie—after you visit the studio? An intimate little family dinner."

"That sounds lovely," Flora answered. "Yes, I'd love to," she repeated to convince herself as much as Maisie. "Thank you—thank you both," she said to her sister as well as Lady Ivers. "I know I've been a rather pathetic bundle of nerves these past weeks."

"Not at'll," Lady Ivers rejoined, as Maisie said. "No more than you have done for me—for years. I am happy to, at least in some small way, re-pay that debt." She came forward in her uneven way to hug her sister. "You will get through this. You will conquer this."

"I hope you are right, but at the moment, I am nothing but regret that I did not do something more."

"What more were you to have done?" Lady Ivers asked.

"I don't know," Flora answered. "Something...*more*. Something that would have kept him with me."

"Well," a deep male voice said. "I'm here with you now."

His voice was so clear and so familiar, it was as if she had conjured him out of her dreams. So real she had to turn around. And stare at the figure in the doorway.

And there he was.

Tall and dashing, however rough and weathered. Water coursed off his hat into his face, even as he belatedly swept it from his head and stood there, dripping upon the carpet.

If at their very first meeting she had seen something weary in the set of his mouth and something sad in the corners of his dark brown eyes, there was now, despite his sodden appearance, nothing but blazing hope.

Flora opened her mouth to speak or scream or do anything but gape at him as if he were a ghost. "Jack." His name was the barest whisper. "You came back."

"Yes. As you see." His smile stretched up one corner of his mouth. "And as I promised."

"Yes." She nodded at him, perhaps a little vehemently. But still, she didn't move—she was afraid to. Afraid her legs would give out from under her. "How have you come? How long can you stay?"

"Well." He put one hand to his hip. "I have come in

the hope that I might take you up on your very generous offer."

Relief, and some far more violent emotion, made her giddy. "My offer to love and keep you for all the rest of your days?"

"Yes, that particular offer, exactly." He nodded but did not come any closer. "But I suppose it's a bad sign that you haven't flown across the room and thrown yourself into my arms. Does this mean you've found someone else in the short time we've been part—"

"Jack." This time, the sound that she made of his name was something more akin to a screech, unmannerly and unladylike. But she did not care. Because she had finally convinced her body to follow her mind's dictates and launched herself across the room like a softer, but no less volatile, cannonball. Because her rogue was home at last. "Jack. Jack. Jack."

Somehow, he absorbed the force of her blow and weathered the storm of her kisses. "Yes, Flora. Yes."

"You came home." She drank in the taste of him, cold and clean. And the smell of him, salt, and rain and still, under all, that hint of starch.

He took her face between his hands. "Yes, Flora, yes."

She kissed him in answer. "Promise me you'll never leave."

"I'll never leave," he vowed.

More kisses in reward. "Never again."

"Never."

She clung to him, holding on to his warm, solid body. Breathing in his rain-dampened, starchy scent. Feeling the rise and fall of his breath within him.

She dashed away tears. "How did you do it?"

"Defeat the Dutch? Well, tactics, primarily. And following Nelson instead of the Admiral. Much more effective Nelson's way."

"I don't care about Nelson."

"Well, that is a surprise. He's the hero of the day," Lady Ivers, who Flora had frankly forgotten in the face of Jack's return.

"I don't care about heroes," Flora told them both. "I care about you."

"Well, that is very good to hear," Jack teased. "Nelson may have gotten the glory, but I have got the girl. I have definitely got the better part of that deal."

"Are you really home for good?"

"Aye," he confirmed by raising her hand to his lips for a kiss. "I am really home for good. If you'll have me."

Relief was like a balm for her soul, easing and exciting her all at the same time. "I'd have it no other way."

"Are you sure you're going to feel that way when I use up all your fortune paying back the earldom's debts?" he asked.

Oh!" She pushed herself away only enough to take his

hands. "As to that, I hope you don't mind, but I've been reorganizing your finances—at least on paper—and I think I have come up with a structure that will allow us to live more comfortably. I've made an offer and renegotiated the loans with the bankers, since I am now one of the principal shareholders of both banks that hold the notes on Kinloch."

He gaped at her. "You've done what?"

"Found my purpose. Better arithmetic," she tried to assure him. "Re-negotiated interest rates. Ensured that the banks will earn a better rate of return refinancing your debt than they would if they bankrupted you."

He was clearly stunned. "I thought they already had —bankrupted me."

"Not entirely. There was room for improvement once I showed them where that room was. I've found my purpose, Jack."

He began to laugh—a strange, coughing sort of nigh-on maniacal laugh.

Flora began to get nervous. "Jack?"

"Do you know," he began, "When you came to my ship in Plymouth Harbor and said you had come to save me, I thought you were mad. Utterly, completely mad. But now I know that it was I who was mad from the beginning. Mad for you. Utterly, completely, delightfully mad."

"Does that mean you are going to marry me?"

"If you'll still have me, yes. As soon as possible. Tomorrow. Today."

"Tuesday next, on Christmas Eve." Flora made up her mind. "So I can get cook to do a proper wedding breakfast. With my sister and my friends there."

"Especially Lady Ivers," put in that lady, who Flora had frankly forgotten in the bliss of her reunion.

"Especially, our Lady Ivers," Flora agreed. "I hope you will stand in the place of mother of the bride, if you will?"

"My dear girl." Lady Ivers came to embrace them both. "I would not have it any other way."

"And I for one wouldn't have it any other way, either."

Jack laughed and kissed Flora's hand, and almost everything was right with the world. What was wrong was that he said, "Well, now that that has been settled, I suppose I ought to take my leave and see my solicitors about opening up my house and—"

Flora grasped at his hand. "You're not leaving? Not so soon? Not just yet." She began to think up excuses, concerns, reasons for him to stay. "Please. I need your help here. I've already made plans for a new house for us. Right in front of yours, in Kings Circus. But it's not quite ready. With the—" Her reason had fled her. Just as it always did in his presence. "Just please don't go," she finished. "I haven't had near enough time just to look at you."

He smiled. His eyes crinkled at the corners and his mouth swept up on one side, and Flora didn't think there was anything else in the world that she had rather see than his dear, smiling face.

"I don't know what I was thinking," he laughed. "I've waited months to be able to come to you and I am damn well not letting go of you now."

"No," Flora agreed. "You are not. You must be with me always."

"Aye, aye," he swore like the sailor he was. "From this moment on. Forgive me, my lady, my sister-to-be." He sketched a brief bow to Lady Ivers and Maisie before he swept Flora up in his arms. "We have pressing business that needs must be attended to this moment…"

And he proceeded to carry her off toward the stair as if she weighed nothing. As if all the weariness of the road and the efforts of travel were nothing to him. "I promise," he whispered into her ear as he took the stairs two at a time, "I shall not waste a moment more."

EPILOGUE

*T*hey were married on that cold Christmas Eve morning, under a blanket of fresh, new snow and a swag of greenery redolent with the scent of laurel, bay, fir, holly, and ivy, like hope in the air.

Jack wore his uniform one last time before he would put it away for good.

Flora wore her deep green velvet—with a new-sewn over-robe of white satin and lace, which Raines had insisted upon for bridal propriety's sake. And instead of a posey of winter flowers, her bouquet was a handful of mistletoe and holly—a portable kissing bough with white and red berries that matched her eyes, which were reddened from crying.

"Don't mind me," she said as she arrived at the altar of St. Andrew's Kirk to stand beside him. "It's only because I'm intolerably happy."

"You have an astonishing way of showing it. But, yes," her darling Jack agreed. "Let's always be this happy."

"Yes," Flora said on a happy sigh, whilst also pulling out a handkerchief and blowing her glowing nose. And still, she had never looked more beautiful. "As long as we're together."

"From now on," he pledged, taking her hand in his.

"Do you promise?"

"Flora, my love, you are in luck—this entire ceremony we are about to undertake shall be nothing but promises to one another."

"Yes, of course," she agreed with a frown that did nothing to mar the perfection of her perfectly oval face. "But I want to make sure, before things get started."

"My divine Flora, perhaps you might consider that things have already started?" He gestured to their surroundings as proof of the fact that they were indeed, at a church, about to pledge their troth to each other.

"Yes, but—"

"Then why don't we simply let the rector begin so we can get to the promising as soon as possible?"

"Yes," that long suffering cleric agreed. "Let's." He cleared his throat to begin without any further delay. "Dearly beloved…"

Jack stood and listened and said what needed to be said, though he felt strangely detached, as if he were watching himself from a great distance. All he could do was hold her hand, so small and fragile looking, and yet so full of steely strength, and marvel at her beauty and her poise and her honesty and her persistence and wonder at his good fortune in having her by his side.

He had never been so happy.

And he had never been luckier. Because he was truly, madly, deeply, and, for the first time in his life, openly in love with his wife.

"Jack, dearest? Are you crying?"

"Only a little. And only because you've made it the fashion. And only because I'm so intolerably happy."

"Yes," she agreed on a sniff. "Just as we bloody well ought to be."

The rector gasped his disapproval, but Jack could only laugh. "I love you, Mrs. Balfour."

"Yes," she smiled up at him, luminous and knowing. "Just as you ought to, my darling Captain. Just as you ought. Happy Christmas, my darling Jack."

"Yes," he answered. "A very Merry Christmas to us."

AUTHOR'S NOTE

This novella follows hard upon the heels of *Mad Rogues and Englishwomen* and concludes my Highland Brides series. I hope you enjoyed seeing old friends from the Highland Brides world—Lady Quince Cairn and her husband Lord Alasdair Cairn from *Mad About the Marquess;* Hamish Cathcart and his wife, Elspeth Otis Cathcart, along with her 'fairy' godmother, Lady Augusta Ivers from *A Fine Madness*; the Duke and Duchess of Crief, Ewan and Greer, from *Mad Plaid & Dangerous to Marry;* and last but not least, Maisie Conway and Archie Carrington from *Mad Rogues and Englishwomen.* (The only Highland Bride we don't see in this novella is Mignon and her husband Rory Cathcart from *Mad for Love.*)

This novella also contains an 'easter egg' of a character from my other romance series, the Reckless

Brides. In that series, our heroes are all Royal Navy men, much like the roguish hero of *A Rogue's Christmas*, Captain Jack Balfour, and many of them are mentored and championed by Sir Charles Middleton, who serves as a 'fairy godfather,' much the way Lady Augusta Ivers acts as fairy godmother for our heroines.

I hope you enjoyed this story of Flora and Jack! Wishing all my readers comfort and joy.

ABOUT THE AUTHOR

ELIZABETH ESSEX is the *USA Today* bestselling author of over twenty critically acclaimed historical romances, including the Reckless Brides and Highland Brides series.

Her books have been nominated for numerous awards, including the Gayle Wilson Award of Excellence, the Romantic Times Reviewers' Choice and Seal of Excellence Awards, and RWA's prestigious RITA Award. The Reckless Brides Series has also made Top-Ten lists from Romantic Times, The Romance Reviews and Affaire de Coeur Magazine, and every book in the series was awarded Desert Isle Keeper status at All About Romance. Her fifth book, A BREATH OF SCANDAL, was named Best Historical in the Reader's Crown 2013.

When not rereading Jane Austen, mucking about in her garden, walking her beloved dogs, Ghillie and Brogue, or simply messing about with boats, Elizabeth can be always be found with her laptop, making up stories about heroes and heroines who live far more exciting lives than she. It wasn't always so.

Long before she ever set pen to paper, Elizabeth graduated from Hollins College with a BA in Classics and Art History, and then earned her MA in Nautical Archaeology from Texas A&M University. While she loved the academic life of an underwater archaeologist, she has found her true calling writing lush, lyrical historical romance full of mystery, passion, daring and adventure.

Elizabeth lives in Texas with her husband, the Indispensable Mr. Essex, and her active and exuberant family in an old house filled to the brim with books.

http://www.elizabethessex.com/

ALSO BY ELIZABETH ESSEX

The Highland Brides

Mad for Love (long novella)

Mad About the Marquess

A Fine Madness (novella)

Mad, Plaid and Dangerous to Marry

Mad Rogues and Englishwomen

A Rogue's Christmas

The Reckless Brides

Almost a Scandal

A Breath of Scandal

After the Scandal

A Scandal to Remember

The Scandal Before Christmas (holiday novella)

A Lady's Gift for Scandal (holiday novella)

The Difference One Duke Makes (novella)

She Walks in Scandal (novella in *A Midsummer Night's Romance* Anthology)

ALSO BY ELIZABETH ESSEX

The Dartmouth Brides

The Pursuit of Pleasure

A Sense of Sin

The Danger of Desire

The Dartmouth Brides Boxed Set (with holiday novella "*Up on the Rooftops*")

The Kent Brothers Chronicles

Between the Devil & the Deep Blue Sea ~ and ~ The Devil's Own Luck

To keep up to date on new releases and events, sign up for Elizabeth's newsletter and get exclusive excerpts, contests and more, visit:

http://www.elizabethessex.com

I also hope you'll take a few minutes out of your day to review this book at your favorite book site – your honest opinion is much appreciated. Reviews help introduce readers to new authors they wouldn't otherwise meet.

Milton Keynes UK
Ingram Content Group UK Ltd.
UKHW030857051124
450766UK00005B/492

9 781648 397257